DANGER IS *STILL* EVERYWHERE

DANGER
IS STILL
EVERYWHERE

BEWARE OF THE DOG!

by **Dr. Noel Zone**
"THE GREATEST DANGEROLOGIST IN THE WORLD, EVER"

A new handbook for avoiding EVEN BIGGER DANGER

With the help of my neighbors
DAVID O'DOHERTY (words)
and **CHRIS JUDGE** (pictures)

LB

Little, Brown and Company
New York Boston

Little, Brown and Company

Hachette Book Group
1290 Avenue of the Americas, New York, NY 10104
Visit us at lb-kids.com

Little, Brown and Company is a division of Hachette Book Group, Inc.
The Little, Brown name and logo are trademarks of Hachette Book Group, Inc.

The publisher is not responsible for websites (or their content)
that are not owned by the publisher.

First U.S. Hardcover Edition: October 2015
Originally published in Great Britain in 2015 by Puffin Books

ISBN 978-0-316-29934-3

Library of Congress Control Number: 2015943551

10 9 8 7 6 5 4 3 2 1

RRD-C
Book design by Chris Judge
Printed in the United States of America

I dedicate this book to my next-door neighbor, Gretel.
I've written this poem for her:

Oh, Gretel, you are so lovely.
Just like a cabbage petal,
You are not dangerous at all,
Unlike a swimsuit made of nettles.

—Dr. Noel Zone

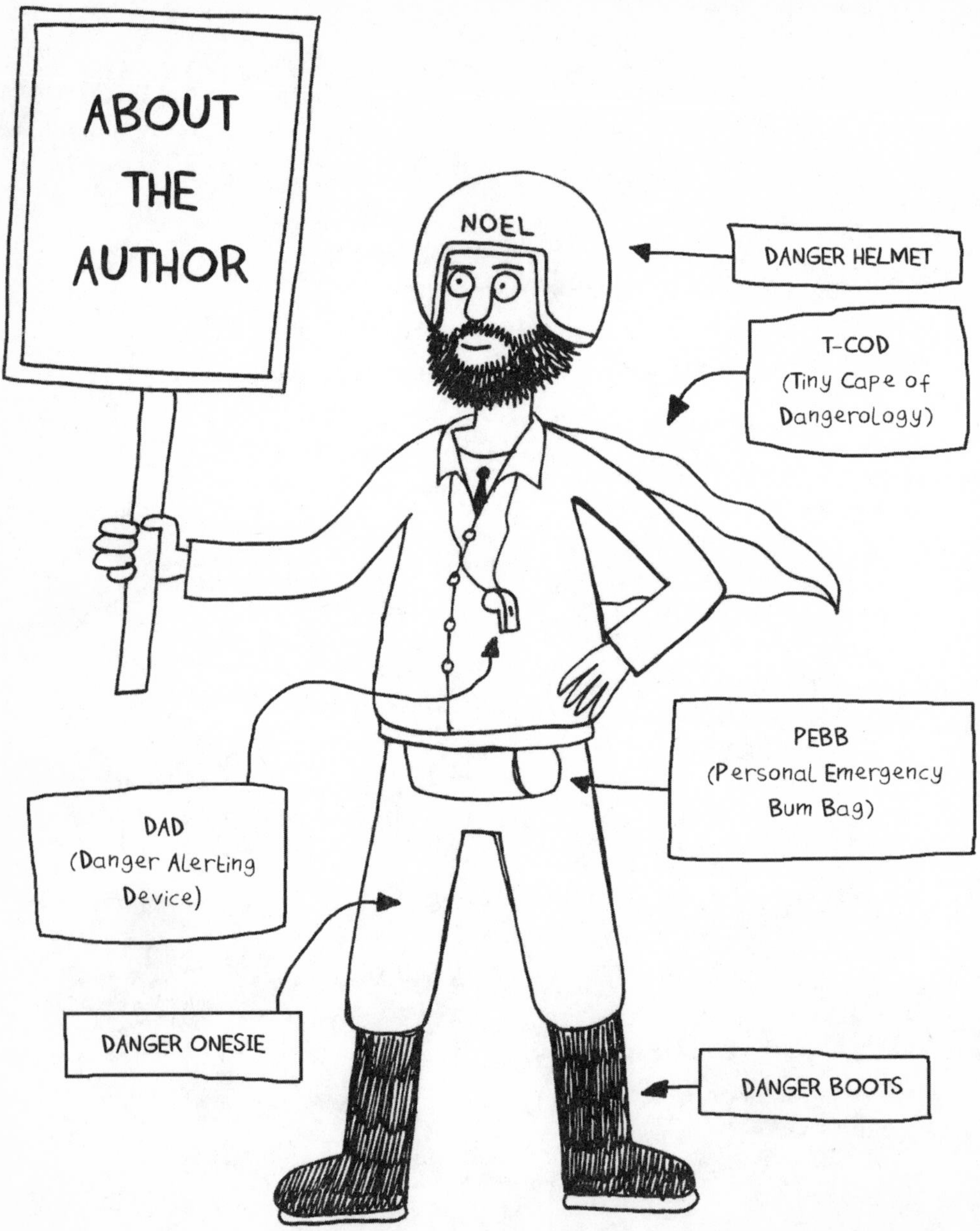
ABOUT THE AUTHOR
NOEL
DANGER HELMET
T-COD (Tiny Cape of Dangerology)
PEBB (Personal Emergency Bum Bag)
DAD (Danger Alerting Device)
DANGER ONESIE
DANGER BOOTS

What word best describes this amazing man?

BRILLIANT! INGENIOUS! STYLISH!

With his magnificent beard shimmering in the sunlight, his **T-COD** fluttering in the breeze, Docter Noel Zone truly is the world's greatest **DANGEROLOGIST** ever.

NOTE: This is definitely true because I invented the word **DANGEROLOGIST.**

What is a **DANGEROLOGIST?** It's a special kind of **HERO** who can spot **DANGER** where nobody else sees any.

Examples of things I regard as

INCREDIBLY DANGEROUS include:

TOAST	PETS	BIRTHDAY CAKE	BICYCLES
(burning)	(chomping)	(fire!)	(EVERYTHING)

Docter Noel Zone lives a **VERY** exciting life in the house he calls

THE DANGERZONE.

It is next door to Gretel, the most beautiful and intelligent person who has ever existed and the talented producer of the

WORLD'S MOST DELICIOUS CABBAGES

(my favorite food).

He wishes he could tell her how he feels, but he always panics when he sees her and says nothing or hides behind something until she has gone. . . .

Oh, Gretel, I just get so flustered!

Gretel is much more beautiful than this.

I CAN'T PRETEND NOT TO BE WRITING THIS ANYMORE.

Gretel, if you ever read this, **PLEASE COME OVER TO THE DANGERZONE.** I'm sure we'd get along so well.

Thank you.

NOTE: I am a **DOCTER** of **DANGEROLOGY,** not a **DOCTOR** of medicine.

There is a **BIG** difference. I can't help you with a brace for your ankle, but I **CAN** help you if you want to know if there is

A VOLCANO UNDERNEATH YOUR HOME.

NOTE 2: I will explain how to tell if there is a volcano underneath your home **SOON.** In the meantime, **STAY CALM AND KEEP READING.**

INTRODUCTION

STOP READING THIS BOOK!

BOOKS ARE VERY DANGEROUS.

No, **WAIT.** You'd better **KEEP READING THIS BOOK**
so I can explain why books are so dangerous, but
BE VERY CAREFUL WHILE YOU DO.

NOTE: If you didn't know that books are very dangerous,
**THEN YOU HAVE A LOT TO LEARN ABOUT
DANGER AND DANGEROLOGY.**

(Which means that you are in the right place, because
**YOU ARE ABOUT TO LEARN A LOT ABOUT
DANGER AND DANGEROLOGY.**)

PREREADING SAFETY CHECKS

Before reading this, or **ANY** book, you must make sure you have all the correct

BRABSE

WHAT IS BRABSE?

Good question! **BRABSE** is short for Book-Reading-And-Browsing Safety Equipment.

NOTE: I'm afraid there will be **A LOT** of abbreviations like that in this book.

we **DANGEROLOGISTS** have so much danger to point out in the world that very often

TITTUFW

(There Isn't Time To Use Full Words).

Basic BRABSE

1. READING GOGGLES

NOEL

Every year, hundreds of people go to the hospital, having been poked in the eye while reading books **THEY DIDN'T REALIZE WERE POP-UP BOOKS.**

Imagine how **AWFUL** that is.

You're reading a book. . . .

"I'm really enjoying this nice book," you're thinking to yourself. . . . "It's just so relaxing and entertaining. . . . I can't wait to turn the page and enjoy more of . . ."

Suddenly your POP-UP book **BOPS YOU IN THE FACE!**
They shouldn't be called POP-UP books. They should be called **EXPLODING TERROR MACHINES.**

3

For things in this book that are Really Awfully Dangerous (RAD),
I will honk the **RAD HORN** to remind you to
PAY SPECIAL ATTENTION.

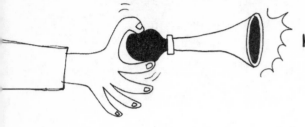

HONK! HONK! HONK!

So, before reading this or **ANY** book,

ALWAYS

ALWAYS

ALWAYS

REMEMBER TO CHECK IF IT IS A POP-UP BOOK.

HOW TO CHECK IF A BOOK IS A POP-UP BOOK

1. Put on your **READING GOGGLES.**

2. With the book facing **AWAY** from you, open each page in front of a soft cushion or pillow. Then, if anything jumps out, the very worst that can happen is the **CUSHION/PILLOW GETS BOPPED.**

3. If nothing pops up, you can **BEGIN READING THE BOOK IMMEDIATELY** or put it into the **TIDNAPUB** (This Is Definitely Not A Pop-Up Book) section of your bookshelf.

TIDNAPUB

WARNING! POP-UP BOOKS! STAY AWAY

WHAT TO DO IF YOU FIND A POP-UP BOOK

1. Dig a very deep hole.

2. Place the book at the bottom of that hole.

3. Fill in the hole.

4. Plant a prickly bush on top of where the hole was.

5. Put a family of very large, angry eagles in that bush so nobody ever goes near it again.

NOTE: READING GOGGLES also protect your book from being splashed by your tears if it is a particularly sad book.

NOTE 2: This is not a sad book, **BUT** you may **CRY WITH TERROR** as some of the things in it are so scary.

For example, there will be a section about bus stops that is really, really terrifying. I won't say anything else about it at the moment because it is **SO SCARY**, it might make you stop reading any more of this book. Ugh, I shouldn't even have mentioned it.

PLEASE TRY TO FORGET WHAT I JUST SAID.

NEWS FLASH!

Another **MASSIVE** danger while reading
is my old nemesis,

THE PAGE 9 SCORPION.

This is a nasty creepy-crawly that
lives in bookstores and libraries.
It likes nothing better than to sneak into
books and lie in wait on page 9. Then, if you're not paying
attention, when you open page 9—it leaps out and attaches
itself to your nose for a year, spraying poison from
its bottom at anyone it doesn't like.

Just a picture, not a real
PAGE 9 SCORPION.

NOTE: THE PAGE 9 SCORPION DOESN'T LIKE ANYONE.

Luckily, I have come up with **AN INGENIOUS PLAN** to outwit
this terrible beast and save your nose.
I have hidden page 9 in another part of this handbook,

a part where, hopefully, **THE PAGE 9 SCORPION** won't be
able to find it. In the meantime, we will continue
straight from page 8 to page 10.

TOO BAD, PAGE 9 SCORPION!

Better Luck **NEVER!**

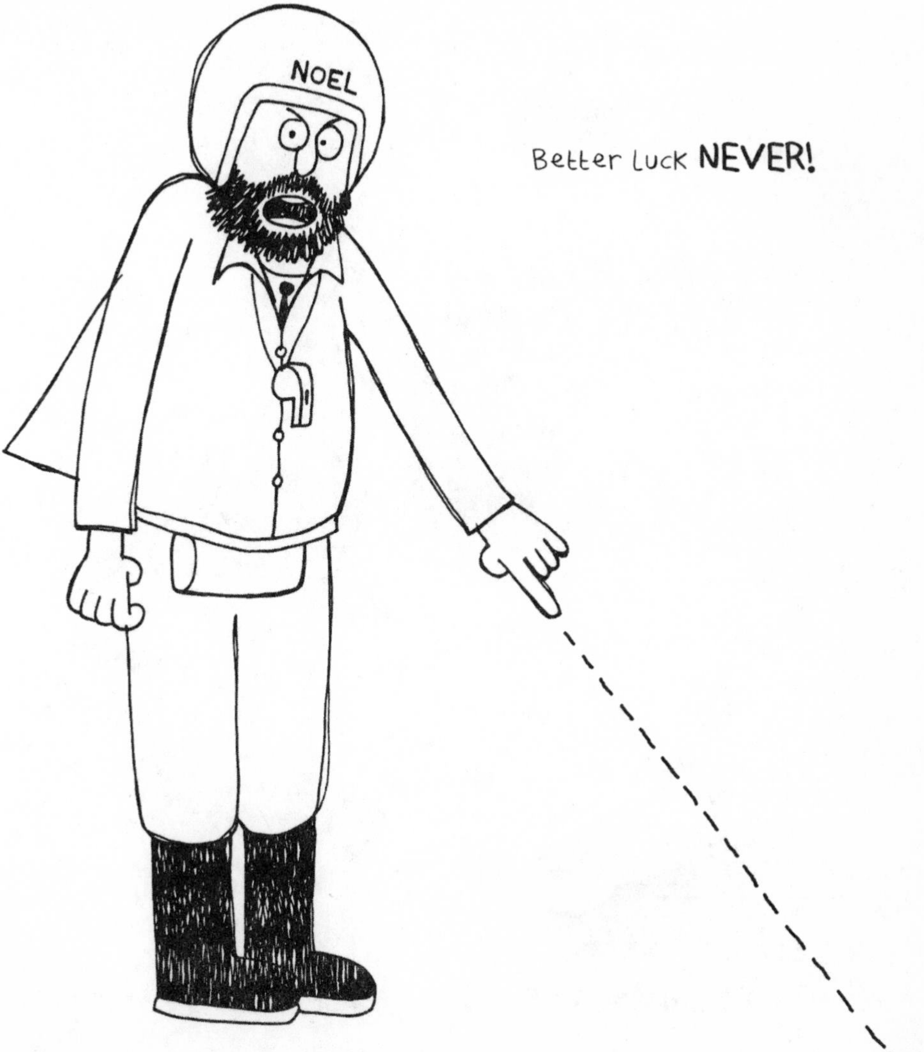
NOEL

Sorry if that last bit about POP-UP books was too scary.
In the future, I will warn you when there is a very scary part
coming up with the **SKULL AND CROSSZONES** symbol:

When you see this symbol **AND** this one

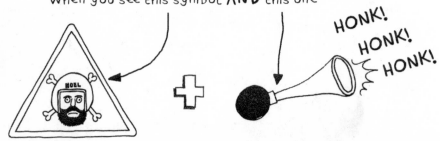

HONK!
HONK!
HONK!

then the next section is going to be very scary
AND REALLY AWFULLY DANGEROUS (RAD).

Thank you.

We were talking about **READING GOGGLES** before
I got distracted. You were probably wondering:

DOCTER NOEL, WHERE DO I GET READING GOGGLES?

Swimming or ski goggles make excellent **READING GOGGLES**,
though personally I choose to read in a snorkel and mask.
These are also useful if there is a sudden flood, or if I am
enjoying a book so much I don't notice where I'm going

AND WALK INTO A RIVER.

NOTE: It's best not to read while you are walking.

NOTE 2: If you wear glasses, you are already protected
from pop-up books, so you could have skipped all of this.
Sorry. I should have said that at the beginning.

Basic **BRABSE** (continued)

2. READING GLOVES

As you can see, books are big and pointy and have **VERY SHARP PAGES.** In many ways, reading a book is like trying to **WRESTLE A HEDGEHOG KANGAROO.**

NOTE: I made up this animal, **BUT I DID IT SO THAT YOU WOULD GET THE IDEA.**

While reading, **ALWAYS WEAR THICK READING GLOVES.**

I like to read in these snazzy oven mitts.

But other stylish options include:

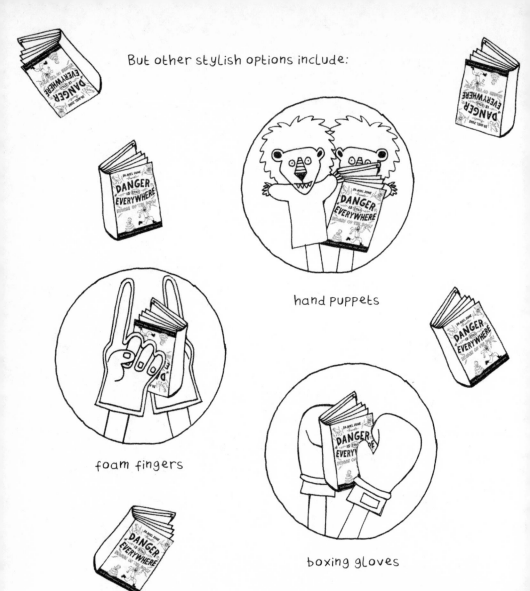

hand puppets

foam fingers

boxing gloves

NOTE 2: Never wear hand puppets that are **TOO** realistic. It will look like **LIONS ARE EATING YOUR BOOK.**

3. DANGER BOOTS

I'm sure you have noticed how heavy this book is. Now think how much it would hurt if you were so shocked or terrified by something in it (for example, the bus-stop part that is coming up later) that the book slipped out of your

READING GLOVES and landed

ON YOUR FOOT.

OW!!

ALWAYS wear protective footwear when reading.
DANGER BOOTS will save you from the most common
BRABIs (Book-Reading-And-Browsing Injuries), including:

COOKBOOK FOOT
You will be very sore as cookbooks are so heavy.

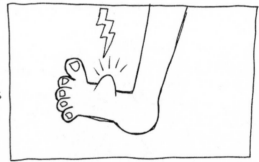

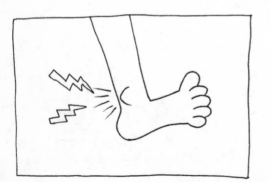

ATLAS ANKLE
You will be even sorer as atlases are **EVEN HEAVIER.**

ENCYCLOPEDIA KNEE

OUCH! These can be
REALLY enormous.

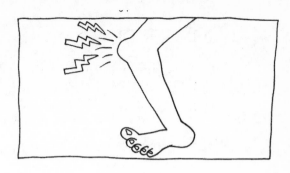

TELEPHONE BOOK LEG

You will need to get
medical help if you drop
one of these on yourself.
But at least
you'll have the
telephone number
of the doctor close by.

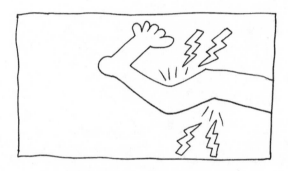

NOTE: In this case, you need a doct**OR**, not a **DOCTER**.

DICTIONARY TOE

The worst **BRABI** of all.
Drop a dictionary on your
toe and I'm certain the
sound you make won't be
in that book.

OWWWWMYYYYTOOOOOEEEEEE!

18

4. A DANGER DEN

I have no doubt you will be **SO FASCINATED AND ENTHRALLED** by this book that you won't notice if dangerous things are happening around you. So it is **VITAL** that you find a **DANGER-FREE** location to read it.

Some suitable places I recommend are:

A. Under a table.

NOTE: Make sure it is a table, and you're not **SITTING UNDERNEATH A HIPPO.**

Bo Inside a piano.

NOTE: AVOID HAUNTED PIANOS.

NOTE 2: You can tell a piano is haunted if every tune you play on it sounds **SCARY**.

Co Inside your own **DANGER-PROOF**
cushion castle/pillow palace/cabbage crib.

EDPUs

(Emergency Danger-Preventing Uses) of

DANGER IS *STILL* EVERYWHERE

Another **VERY IMPORTANT** thing before we start: While this book is meant to be read, it has other excellent **EDPUs** you should be aware of.

1. A TINY ISLAND

Suppose you have forgotten to wear your **DANGER BOOTS** and suddenly find yourself stuck in the middle of a very small flood. And worse—you look down and see that

THE FLOOD IS FULL OF TINY PIRANHAS.

Then this book could be used as an emergency tiny island.

NOTE: This will ruin your book, but could save your feet.

2. A VERY SMALL LADDER

Need to see over a hedge that is just a tiny bit taller than you are?
Maybe to check for dangerous animals/neighbors/a volcano?
 You can use this book to do that.

WARNING: DO NOT PLACE MORE THAN TWO COPIES
ON TOP OF EACH OTHER. That would create a

DANGER IS ⭐STILL⭐ **EVERYWHERE** MOUNTAIN that

you could easily topple off.

3. AN EMERGENCY DANGER HELMET

Imagine you are caught outside without your

DANGER HELMET and it starts to hail.

Or worse—**IT STARTS TO RAIN DOWN BIRD POOP.**

Then you can balance this book on your head and use it as a temporary replacement danger helmet/poop shield.

NOTE: I, Docter Noel Zone, am **NOT** responsible

for removing the bird poop from your copy of

DANGER IS STILL **EVERYWHERE** if this happens.

4. A DISGUISE

Find yourself in a dangerous situation and need to pretend to be someone else? Simply turn to the next page and hold this book in front of your face. Then everyone will think you are me.

NOTE: Please don't use this disguise if you have done something really, really bad. Because then I **WILL GET THE BLAME.**

NOTE 2: Please don't use this disguise if I am around. It will be **VERY** confusing for me.

NOTE 3: DEFINITELY DON'T USE THIS DISGUISE IF GRETEL IS AROUND.

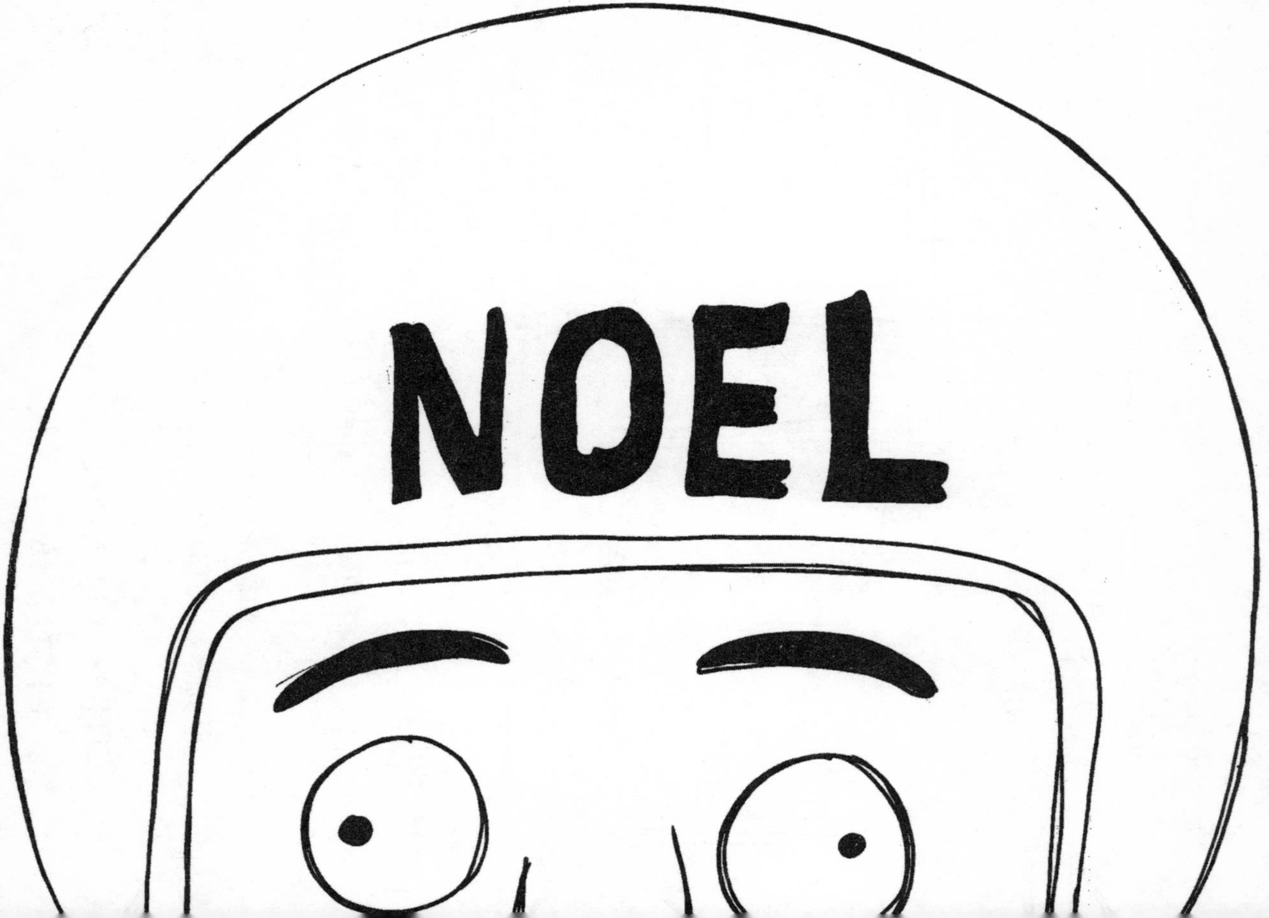
NOEL

5. DANGER TONGS

Need to pick up something dangerous, such as a very pointy carrot, a bunch of keys, **OR A HORRIBLY SMELLY SOCK?**

In an emergency situation, you can use this book to do that.

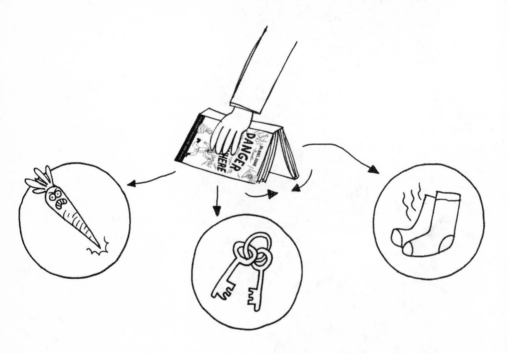

NOTE: After a stinky-sock lift, **YOU SHOULD PROBABLY LEAVE THIS BOOK OUTSIDE IN THE FRESH AIR FOR A WHILE.**

6. Other less dangerous uses of this book include:

a toast rack,

a kennel for a small pet stone (the best pet),

or a fan—useful if you want to dry your hair very slowly.

Finally, **WHAT IS THE POINT OF THIS BOOK?**

I thought you'd never ask. The **MAIN AIM** of this book is to prepare you for the

LEVEL 2 DETBAFOD

(Dangerology Examination To Become A Full-On Dangerologist).

Having made it **THIS FAR** you are already a Level 2 **POD**

(Pupil Of Dangerology).

But if you make it all the way to the end of the book and then answer all the questions at the back correctly you will become a

Level 2 **FOD**

(Full-On Dangerologist).

HOWEVER, if you get any of those questions wrong, then I'm afraid you will have to

START THE
BOOK ALL OVER
AGAIN!

And if you keep getting questions wrong **YOU WILL HAVE TO KEEP READING IT OVER AND OVER FOR THE REST OF YOUR LIFE** (which would be fine for a while, as it's quite an exciting book, but even I admit it would get a bit repetitive around the five- or six-hundredth time).

Sorry about that, **BUT THOSE ARE THE RULES.**

So good luck, Level 2 **PODs**, and please be careful as we begin:

WELCOME to **DANGER** IS ⟨STILL⟩ **EVERYWHERE,**

my brand-new handbook for avoiding danger and awful

things in the world. My name is **DOCTER NOEL ZONE.**

I should note at this point that I am a person and **NOT** a wardrobe.

NOTE: I like to give all of my furniture names. This wardrobe is called **GORDON.**

So, to recap, I am **NOT A WARDROBE** but a man called Docter Noel Zone hiding inside a wardrobe called Gordon, which is here in my bathroom. Look, my hand is doing a little wave out the door. If I hold my hand still, you can give me a **SHY FIVE.**

STOP THIS BOOK!

I've just realized that this has been a very confusing start.

I suspect, even though we've only just begun, you are already baffled by at least three things. So let me answer what I'm guessing are the main questions you have.

QUESTION 1: Why is there a wardrobe in your bathroom, Docter Noel?

QUESTION 2: Docter Noel, why are you inside this wardrobe?

QUESTION 3: WHAT ON EARTH IS A SHY FIVE?

GOOD QUESTIONING!

With questioning like this, you will make an excellent

Level 2 **FOD**. That is, of course, if you aren't too terrified by bits like the bus-stop part—sorry, I shouldn't have mentioned it again—and manage to make it all the way to the end of the book.

Back to your questions. I will answer the third question first.

QUESTION 3: WHAT ON EARTH IS A SHY FIVE?

A **SHY FIVE** is a secret, nondangerous way for Level 2
PODS and **FODS** to greet each other. It is similar to a
HIGH FIVE, but **MUCH** less dangerous.

People love to **HIGH-FIVE**, but they never stop to think about
**THE AWFUL THINGS THAT COULD HAPPEN
WHILE HIGH-FIVING.**

SOME AWFUL THINGS THAT COULD HAPPEN WHILE HIGH-FIVING

1. You miss your friend's hand and **HIGH-FIVE** him **IN THE FACE.**

Coconut

2. You miss his hand and instead **HIGH-FIVE** a coconut tree, and suddenly coconut monkeys, coconuts, and a pirate who was taking a nap in the coconut tree all fall down around you.

Coconut monkey

Pirate

3. You miss the other person's hand and slap a very angry wrestler who happens to be standing next to him at the bus stop.

4. You don't miss, but your friend didn't want a **HIGH FIVE** because he is holding his pet frog. So what you hear are the three sounds **THWACK**, **CROAK**, and **SPLAT** all at the same time. It sounds like this:

THWOAKSPLAT

(which is the very worst sound for any frog to hear, or perhaps not hear, because they have already been **THWOAKSPLATed**).

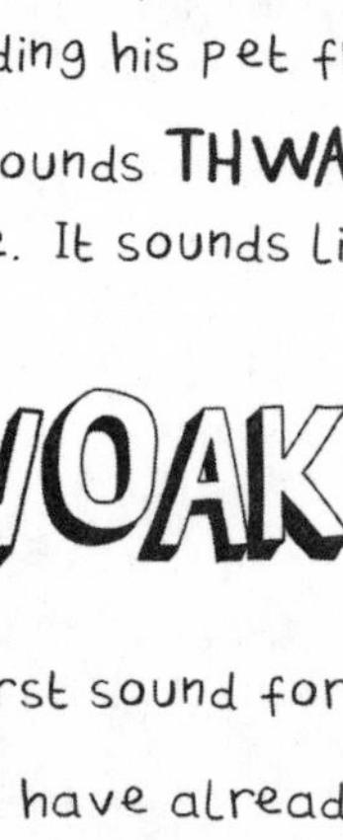

5. You do the **HIGH FIVE** perfectly, but the **THWACK** is so loud it startles a nearby spider catcher. She drops the huge jar of hairy spiders she has been collecting, and it smashes and all the spiders escape. This is particularly bad if you are wearing a fly costume as huge hairy spiders love to chomp big juicy flies.

HOW TO DO A SHY FIVE

1. Both **DANGEROLOGISTS** raise a hand and start to bring them together, exactly as you would in a **HIGH FIVE**.

2. But just when you are about to **THWACK**, just before you touch at all, you stop.

3. Instead of **THWACKING**, you both say "**DANGER**" to remind each other that **DANGER IS STILL EVERYWHERE**.

Thank you.

SHY-FIVE PRACTICE AREA

Before trying it out on other dangerologists, you can practice your **SHY FIVES** on my hand on this page.

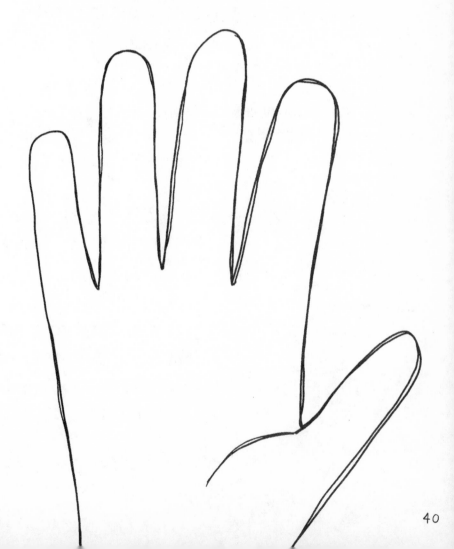

I will answer **QUESTION 1** next:

WHY IS THERE A WARDROBE IN YOUR BATHROOM?

There is a wardrobe in my bathroom because my bathroom
is my bedroom, as I—like most sensible people—sleep in the bathtub

WHY DO YOU SLEEP IN THE BATHTUB?

Good questioning again! There are **SO** many good reasons to
sleep in the bathtub. Here are my top five:

1. You can't fall out of a bathtub.

2. There are no mattress springs that
could go **BOING** underneath
you **AND FIRE YOU THROUGH
THE WINDOW INTO THE
GIRAFFE ENCLOSURE OF THE
ZOO NEXT DOOR.**

NOTE: I live behind the giraffe
enclosure of the zoo.

41

3. You don't have to go far if you need to use the toilet/ brush your teeth.

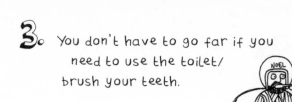

4. You don't have to go far if you want to take a bath. In fact, you don't have to go anywhere.

5. If there is a flood while I am asleep, the bathtub will float like a boat, and I can row away.

REMEMBER, always keep oars beside your bathtub-bed/boat.

NOTE: I call my bathtub-bed/boat **GEORGE**.

Finally, **QUESTION 2:**

<u>WHY ARE YOU INSIDE A WARDROBE?</u>

To answer this question, we will need to go back in time. And I mean even further back than yesterday, when I started spending a lot of time inside this wardrobe.

Even further back than when this wardrobe was built
(and Gordon is quite an old wardrobe).

Back before this house was built. Or this street. Or **ANY** street.

Back before there were any people on this planet
or animals walking around on it.

We need to go back to a time, hundreds of millions of years ago, when there were only sponges.

The sea was full of them, swimming around, bumping into one another. Well, not really bumping, because sponges don't bump. They just gently sponge.

Why have I gone all the way back to this time?

BECAUSE THIS IS WHEN I WOULD
MOST LIKE TO HAVE LIVED.

It was a time when there was **NO DANGER.**

I mean, what's the worst thing that can happen when there are just sponges?

CORRECT ANSWER: Nothing. You might get washed a little bit by accident.

Fast forward a few hundred million years and the problems start.

Danger was invented by the dinosaurs. They were enormous and clumsy and loud and pointy. On top of that, they got angry **VERY** easily.

Simon and Buckles, two raptors, would be out for a romantic meal when suddenly—

PLOP—their waiter Rory (a T. rex) would trip over his huge feet, and the huge pudding they had ordered would land on their heads.

Then a passing pterodactyl (called Terri) would look down and see the pudding party and would swoop in to take some.

But, being clumsy, Terri the pterodactyl would miss and knock into a sunbathing triceratops called Sara, bursting her air mattress. Sara the triceratops would be furious, and soon there would be a huge food fight with all the dinosaurs and the contents of the entire dessert cart.

AND SO . . .

DANGER WAS BORN.

Once the dinosaurs invented danger, the world didn't start getting any less dangerous. Soon there were:

SHARKS

BEARS

WASPS

VIKINGS

CARNIVALS

BICYCLES

POP-UP BOOKS

and other incredibly dangerous things

Fast forward to **YESTERDAY**, and the danger that Rory the T. rex began reached **THE MOST DANGEROUS LEVEL IT HAS EVER BEEN.**

Let me tell you what happened. . . .

THE DAY THAT DANGER
CAME TO THE DANGERZONE

It had been a nice but chilly Sunday morning. I'd had a delicious cabbage for breakfast and taken Dennis, my pet stone **(THE SAFEST PET)**, for a walk around the mattress superstore **(A VERY SAFE WALK)**.

On our way home, I'd spotted Gretel at the bottle-recycling plant, and as usual, instead of saying hello, I panicked and hid behind a tree until she had dropped everything off and gone home. **I WISH I DIDN'T ALWAYS DO THIS.**

Gretel is **MUCH** prettier than this.

Then at the park we stopped to read an
UNBELIEVABLY STUPID SIGN.

JUST ONE WEEK UNTIL THE
PET-OF-THE-YEAR TALENT CONTEST

Think you've got the best pet?
NOW IS YOUR CHANCE TO PROVE IT!
Calling all dancing dogs, cycling cats, poet parrots

ENTER TODAY!
☆ SURPRISE CELEBRITY HOST ☆

Ugh. What a terrible event! As if pets weren't dangerous enough already, some people have taught them how to do other, **PROBABLY EVEN MORE DANGEROUS THINGS.**

Oh great, here's a scary pet lizard. How about

WE SHOW IT HOW TO FLY AN AIRPLANE?

This pet rat is in no way scary enough already, so let's

DRESS IT UP AS A VAMPIRE.

These people obviously don't know that STONES ARE THE BEST (AND SAFEST) PETS.

A STONE :

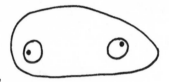

1. Doesn't pee everywhere/anywhere.

2. Doesn't eat your stuff.

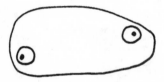

3. Doesn't keep you awake with woofing/meowing/ whatever sound your pet makes.

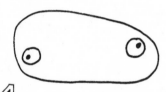

4. Doesn't always/ever want its dinner.

5. Leaves you alone to get on with your **DANGEROLOGY**.

53

As we made our way home, I was looking forward to a nice, quiet evening with Dennis, making **WARNING** signs to put up around the area.

CYCLISTS: Please throw your bikes into this river.

WARNING: LEAVES SOMETIMES FALL FROM THIS TREE!

BEE ALERT! A BEE HAS BEEN SPOTTED IN THIS AREA!

CYCLING IS MUCH TOO DANGEROUS!

STAY AWAY FROM THE PET-OF-THE-YEAR TALENT CONTEST!

Note: Please check that there are no canoeists going by in the river first.

But the moment we arrived home, **EVERYTHING CHANGED.**

There was a large box sitting on the front step.

NOEL, NOEL, THE HAIRY SAUSAGE ROLL!!!!

"Maybe it's the new **DANGER HELMET** I ordered," I thought to myself. "Or a delivery of cabbages. **OR MAYBE SOMEBODY HAS LEFT ME A PRESENT!** How exciting!"

QUESTION: COULD I HAVE BEEN ANY MORE WRONG?

ANSWER = **No × 1,000,000**

There was an envelope stuck to the top of the box, and looking at the name written on it, I immediately knew who it was from.

There is only one person who calls me that: **JOAN.**

HONK!
HONK!
HONK!

I don't think there has ever been a twin brother and sister as different as Noel and Joan Zone. She works as a stuntwoman in movies. She is always telling me how much fun she had skydiving off a mountain or riding one of her motorcycles through something that is on fire.

Joan is, and always has been, the opposite of a

DANGEROLOGIST.

I nervously opened the envelope.

HI, BRO!

Guess what??? Too late, you snail!!!
I won a vacation on the radio this
morning!!!!

Woohoooo!!! You had to call in and say
what the mystery sound was, and I knew
it was a cabbage being hit with a tennis
racket!

Lucky I hit so many of your cabbages
over the wall with my tennis racket
when we were little! Hahaha!!!!!

Anyway, back in seven days.

Oh, nearly forgot. There's something
here I need you to look after. I know
you haven't always gotten along with
her, but I'm sure in a week's time
you'll be besties!!

Love,

Your sis,
Joan Zone

I froze with fear.

"Oh no. No, no, no. No, no, no, no, no."

Then I yelled, **"NOOOOOOOOO!"** And from inside the box the dreadful sound began.

YAP-YAP
YAP-YAP
YAP-YAP

Inside that box was a travel kennel, and inside that was
a tiny twenty-four-hour
nonstop

yap-yapping

never-napping

shoe-chewing

pee- and poop-doing

havoc machine

called . . .

NAPKIN.

If I am the opposite of Joan, then Napkin is the opposite of Dennis.

Dennis realized this the moment I opened the kennel, and Napkin
barged out, did some yap-yapping at nothing in particular, and

began chomping the side of my **DANGER BOOT.**
Then she spotted Dennis and aimed a long, powerful pee in his direction
before sitting directly on top of him and yap-yapping some more.

Whether Dennis liked it or not, Napkin
had found a new best friend.

Whether I liked it or not,

DANGER HAD COME TO
THE DANGERZONE.

So that is the very long answer to **QUESTION 2: WHY ARE YOU INSIDE A WARDROBE?**

A shorter answer would have been: "I am inside Gordon so I can get through all the **VITAL DANGEROLOGY** to prepare you for your Level 2 **DETBAFOD.**"

Or an even shorter one would have been:

X-ray of wardrobe

NOEL

AAAGH! MY HOME HAS BEEN TAKEN OVER BY MY WORST NIGHTMARE!

But we must **KEEP GOING,** Level 2 **PODS!** we have **SO MUCH INCREDIBLY IMPORTANT DANGEROLOGY** in front of us.

GOOD LUCK TO YOU.

(Please wish me luck here also.)

Thank you.

Now let's begin your Level 2 **DANGEROLOGY** education the only way it can possibly begin in these difficult circumstances:

DOG DANGER

Before letting **ANY** dog into your home, you need to answer
THE BIG QUESTION:

IS THIS DOG DEFINITELY A DOG?

AWFUL, AWFUL things will happen if your
dog is not a real dog.

1. ROBOT DOGS

PROBLEM: A robot dog will act like a normal dog until you fall asleep. Then it will sneak into your bedroom/bathroom and pick you up by the pajamas/undies/**DANGER ONESIE** in its **VERY STRONG** robot jaws. Then, using its paw rockets, it will take you back to its **ROBOT-DOG PLANET**, where it and all the other robot dogs will make you throw special **ROBOT STICKS** for them **ALL DAY, EVERY DAY** until your arm **EVENTUALLY FALLS OFF FROM TIREDNESS.**

HOW TO CHECK IF YOUR DOG IS A ROBOT

A simple test—hold a magnet up against your dog.

NAPKIN! Stand still. I'm trying to check if . . . . **STOP TRYING TO EAT THE MAGNET.**

Napkin is **NOT** a robot dog.

2. WOLVES/WEREWOLVES

PROBLEM: Although they look similar to ordinary dogs, **NEVER** let a wolf or werewolf into your home. In no time, it will attract other wolves/werewolves, and they will make **YOU** join their pack and roam around the area, eating chickens and joggers.

HOW TO CHECK IF YOUR DOG IS A WOLF/WEREWOLF

Wait until nighttime and point your dog at the moon. If it goes **YAP-YAP** or **WOOF** or stays silent because it is confused why you are pointing it at the moon, then **GOOD.** ### THAT IS **DEFINITELY A DOG.**

However, if it goes **HOOOOOWL**, then I'm afraid it is **NOT** a dog. **CONTACT YOUR LOCAL WOLF ZOO OR WEREWOLF-CATCHING SERVICE.**

3. ZOMBIE DOGS

PROBLEM: The scariest of all.

No matter how friendly they act,

ZOMBIE DOGS really just
want to chomp you and eat your brain

so that **YOU WILL BECOME
A ZOMBIE, TOO**.

HOW TO CHECK IF YOUR DOG IS A ZOMBIE DOG

Easy. There are two big giveaways with zombie dogs.

A. They walk like zombies, on their back two legs with their paws
sticking out in front.

B. They make this sound: **"UUUUUUH UUUUUUUH"** all day.

NOTE: If your dog is a zombie, take it to the vet, and they can
give it Zom-Be-Gone, the single-dose cure for zombie dogs.

She may not be any of these things, but
**NAPKIN IS STILL VERY
DANGEROUS!**

NAPKIN UPDATE

Already Napkin is causing lots of trouble in **THE DANGERZONE**.

So far, she has chomped one

DANGER BOOT
(luckily I have some spares) and
three cabbages and chewed on

my **DANGER HELMET** while I was taking a nap.
Oh, and she keeps taking the end of the
toilet paper roll off Mr. Chomsky and
winding it around the house like an
enormous tail.

NOEL

NOTE: This never happens with a pet stone.

NOTE 2: Mr. Chomsky is the name of my
toilet-paper-roll dispenser.

But right now she has taken Dennis out to

THE DANGERYARD
(that is what I call my yard)
to help her yap-yap at things outside. So now is a good time for me
to tell you about a **VITAL** piece of **LEVEL 2 DANGEROLOGY**
that you should remember to check **EVERY DAY**.

HONK! HONK! HONK!

Volcanoes are huge underground farts that shoot boiling rocks and earth (and anything else that happens to be down there) up into the air. On a danger scale of kittens to Lions, volcanoes are even more dangerous than Lions. They are as dangerous as robot Lions.

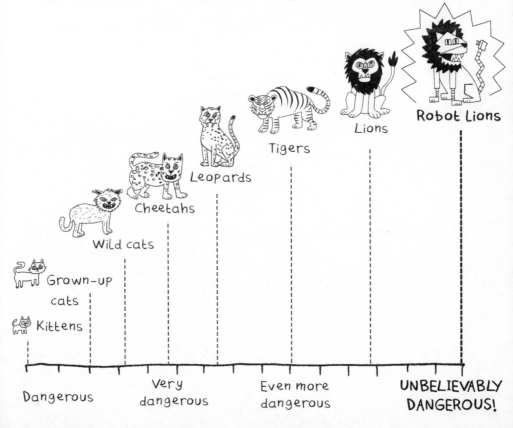

Robot Lions

Lions

Tigers

Leopards

Cheetahs

Wild cats

Grown-up cats

Kittens

Dangerous   Very dangerous   Even more dangerous   UNBELIEVABLY DANGEROUS!

YOU REALLY, REALLY, REALLY DON'T WANT A VOLCANO TO ERUPT UNDERNEATH YOUR HOME, and I can't say **"REALLY"** enough times there. It will fire you and all your stuff up into the air, and when you land it will be in lava, which will melt you like ice cream landing in very hot soup. This is a frightening and also disgusting thought.

NOTE: If you get stuck in a volcano eruption, it's best to sit in your bathtub and try to row away.

(ANOTHER GREAT REASON TO SLEEP IN THE BATHTUB.)

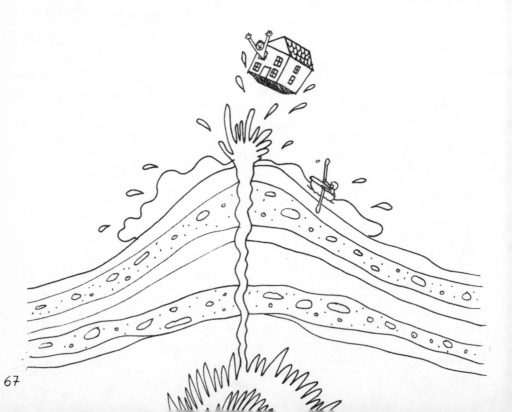

HOW TO CHECK IF A VOLCANO IS ABOUT TO ERUPT UNDERNEATH YOUR HOME

The telltale signs you need to look out for are:

1. SMOKE RISING FROM THE YARD

But make sure this isn't the neighbors having a barbecue.

Remember, **VOLCANOES DON'T SMELL BARBECUEY.**

It's always a good idea to call over the wall to your neighbors,

"EXCUSE ME, IS THIS A BARBECUE OR A VOLCANO?"

NOTE: If you are not quite tall enough to see into your neighbors' yard, remember **YOU CAN USE YOUR COPY OF DANGER IS** (STILL) **EVERYWHERE**.

NOTE 2: Do NOT try to row away from a volcano on your book, though. That would be a bad idea.

2. A REALLY WARM HOME

And I don't mean warm like somebody has left the heat on. I mean **ALWAYS** warm like **AAAAGH, WHY IS THIS SAUSAGE COOKING WHEN I DROP IT ON THE FLOOR?**

3. VERY LOUD RUMBLING

Volcanoes rumble for quite a long time before they go **BOOM**, so you **MUST** be able to check for this.

NOTE: Be careful not to confuse volcano rumbling with a train going by (if you live beside train tracks), the washing machine, or giraffes running around in the zoo behind your home.

NOTE 2: This last one probably only applies to me.

HOW TO CHECK FOR RUMBLING

Go to the lowest part of your home, then just lie on the floor, like I am doing now. Put your ear to the ground and listen. . . .

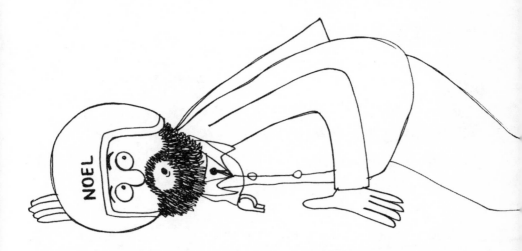

Oh dear, Napkin has come in and now all I can hear is yap-yapping. Napkin, please be quiet for a minute, I'm trying to carry out some **VERY IMPORTANT DANGEROLO**—great, now she's chewing on my **DANGER BOOT. GET AWAY, NAPK**—now she's trying to chomp my **DANGER HELMET** again! Oh good, she's turning around. . . . Wait . . . **AAAAAAGH! DON'T PEE ON ME, NAPKIN!**

Writing this book with Napkin in **THE DANGERZONE** is proving more difficult than I anticipated. Even worse than the chomping and the mess is the noise. Napkin has a very high-pitched yap-yap that sounds like a car alarm.

TOP THREE THINGS THAT NAPKIN YAP-YAPS AT

1. THE GIRAFFES

For once, I agree with Napkin.

THEY ARE VERY ANNOYING.

The way they stare into the **DANGERYARD** all day, chewing on leaves. It's always the same: **CHEW-CHEW-CHEW, STARE-STARE-STARE.** With those long necks and their Ping-Pong-ball eyes.

But yap-yapping doesn't get rid of them. Nothing does. I've even tried dressing up as a lion to try to scare them away. You just have to ignore them.

YOU LOOK LIKE DONKEYS THAT GOT STUCK IN VACUUM CLEANERS.

YAP-YAP YAP-YAP

2. ETHEL

Gretel's cat, Ethel, sits on the wall all day in her tiny cowboy hat, hissing at whatever is going on in **THE DANGERZONE**. As you know, I think everything to do with Gretel is **GREAT**, except Ethel. Ethel is very annoying.

HSSSSSSSSSS...

3. ME

I'm not sure if it's my helmet or my beard or my **DANGER ONESIE** or **DANGER BOOTS**, but every time Napkin is near me it's the same. Even as I write this, she is sitting outside Gordon, yap-yapping and scraping on his door.

YAP-YAP
YAP-YAP

NOTE: This never happens with a pet stone.

I am worried that this handbook of **DANGEROLOGY** is turning into a handbook of **NAPKINOLOGY**. So I will try to block her out by thinking of **AN EVEN SCARIER CREATURE** that every Level 2 **POD** should be ready for.

AAAAaAAA

(Advice About Avoiding Angry and Aggressive Animal Attacks)

THE PUDDLE SHARK

You're strolling to school or to visit a friend or to exercise a dog

that has just eaten another one of your **DANGER BOOTS**.
Up ahead is a puddle. Not a huge one—not one so big that you have
to go around it, but not so small that you can tiptoe through it.

"I know what I'll do," you say to no one in particular.
"I'll just jump over that."

HONK! HONK! HONK!

NO!

NOEL

If you think that's a good idea, then you don't know about
THE PUDDLE SHARK—a nasty, devious, and **EXTREMELY**
HUNGRY beast that lurks in dark puddles of a certain size.

As soon as you try to leap over it,
THE PUDDLE SHARK STRIKES.

And, when I say "strikes," **I MEAN "CHOMPS."**

74

Remember to look out for the telltale signs of the

PUDDLE SHARK.

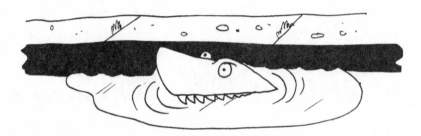

1. Beady eyes peeping out from the water.

2. A pointy fin poking out of it.

3. Clothes, backpacks, and dog leashes floating on the surface, belonging to unlucky

PWINAPODs

(Person Who Is Not A Pupil Of Dangerology)

WHO DIDN'T KNOW ABOUT THE PUDDLE SHARK, EITHER.

VERY CALM NOTIFICATION

Although we are nearly one hundred pages away from it, I feel I should warn you about what may or may not happen on page 145.

You see, some people think I am an annoying busybody who should keep his nose out of their business. And some of those people aren't people. **THEY ARE GHOSTS.** ⟶

To try to stop me from doing my **DANGEROLOGY**, and to stop you from learning it, ghosts have been looking for copies of my books and writing spooky **GHOST GRAFFITI** all over page 145.

NOTE: They choose page 145 because it's their favorite number to say. They say it like this:

The reason I mention this now is just so you are prepared if this has happened in your book. Hopefully it hasn't and you can forget that I ever said this.

Thank you.

NAPKIN STOPS YAP-YAPPIN'

It's a miracle! I've found a way to stop Napkin yap-yapping.
But the problem is that the way to stop her from doing it

MIGHT BE EVEN MORE ANNOYING THAN
THE YAP-YAPPING.

It happened this afternoon. My nieces **Katherine** and **Millicent**
came over after school and took Napkin for a walk into town,
where she almost peed on a crossing guard and then tried
to eat a statue. But they made sure they were back at

THE DANGERZONE in time to watch their favorite TV show.

"It's Max Wurst," Millicent explained. "You must know Max Wurst, Uncle Noel. He's the bravest man on Earth." I hadn't heard of him.

"What sort of brave things does he do? Does he point out where danger is?"

"No," said Millicent. "He does not do that."

Napkin was in the kitchen, trying to put Dennis into the washing machine, when the show began.

Hi, I'm Max Wurst and welcome to **EXPECT THE WURST.**

It wasn't a good start. He was going down a zip line in a dangerous jungle with no shirt on and something dangling around his neck.

"What's that hanging off him? It could easily catch on someth—

IS THAT A SNAKE?"

"Yes! It's his sidekick, Noodle," Katherine told me. "He goes everywhere with Max."

No! No, no, no. I did **NOT** like this show at all, and it had barely

begun. Then the theme music started and it got **EVEN WORSE.**

  "When he sees danger
He dives in headfirst.
He's Max-Max-Max-Max-
Max-Max-Max-Max Wurst."

As I covered my ears, Napkin thundered in from the kitchen, yap-yapping furiously. But the moment she saw Max Wurst, she skidded to a halt and stopped making a sound. She calmly sat down, tilted her head to the side, and began staring at the television. Napkin was mesmerized by this **IDIOT.**

Then, when he got to the bottom of the zip line, he grabbed the head of his snake **AND BLEW INTO IT.** Yes, you did just read that. **HE BLEW INTO A SNAKE!**

"Hi, adventure lovers! It's me, the bravest man on Earth, and I'm here to push danger to its very limits."

"PUSH DANGER TO ITS VERY LIMITS"?
HE ACTUALLY SAID THAT!

As Napkin gazed on adoringly, Max Wurst continued his awfulness.

"This week, I've come here to the jungle to break-dance on a rhino

and twang a sleeping lion's whiskers like a guitar!"

OH MY GOODNESS.

"LET'S DO THIS THING!" he said, before blowing into the snake again.

Katherine and Millicent cheered with delight, and Napkin moved even closer to the television.

By the time the episode ended, I was in a state of shock. I had seen dangerous things I'd never even imagined before.

This Wurst ninny had piggybacked on a gorilla,

Pulled a leopard's tail,

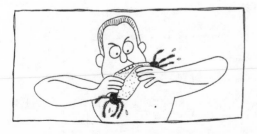

and eaten a tarantula in a burrito.

"Well, that is an individual I never want to be near," I said.
"Too bad," said Katherine excitedly. "He's coming to the park
on Saturday!"

"WHAT?"

Millicent was delighted, too. "He's hosting Pet-of-the-Year!"

My nieces **HIGH-FIVED** each other, but I was too shocked by the

news I just heard to point out **HOW DANGEROUS THAT WAS**

and explain about the **SHY FIVE**.

I could barely speak. "Th-th-that turnip is coming **TO THIS ROAD?"**

"Isn't that so cool?" said Katherine.

"No! It's not cool at all, Katherine. Besides, he doesn't know

anything about pets. He doesn't know anything about **ANYTHING!**"

"Maybe you should enter with Dennis, Uncle Noel. You're always telling us that stones are the best pets," said Millicent. "This would be your chance to show everyone."

"There is about as much chance of me entering that competition with Dennis as there is of Max Wurst taking a bath in George," I said.

We were interrupted by Napkin, who, once the show was over, had begun yap-yapping again. Although these yap-yaps were slightly muffled as she had become stuck in the trash can.

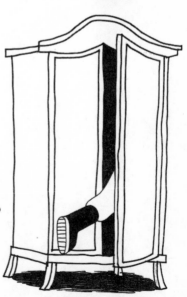

After Katherine and Millicent went home to do their homework, I retreated into Gordon.

I had my own homework to do: writing the

INCREDIBLY IMPORTANT

DANGEROLOGY lessons to get

you **PODs** ready for the

Level 2

DETBAFOD.

As you know, I like to look at the world and tell others how to make it **LESS DANGEROUS.** But I also like to look at the past and tell others how I would have made dangerous times in history **MUCH SAFER.**

So join me in my **DANGEROLOGY TIME MACHINE** (Gordon) for a section I call:

Danger was Every-where

For our first journey through time,
we travel back to **MEDIEVAL TIMES.**

It was an era of knights on horses, princesses in pointy hats, and fire-breathing beasts.

WHERE DOES A DANGEROLOGIST EVEN START?

1. **CASTLES** were much too big and cold and had too many corners you could bang your knee on. I would have made them much smaller and more cushiony. **CORRECT.** I'd have replaced all castles with **BOUNCY CASTLES**. This would have made battles **LESS DANGEROUS** and **MORE FUN**.

YIPPEE!

2. To avoid bursting your castle, all pointy things would have been banned.

The only armor allowed would be **KNITTED ARMOR** and all weapons would be replaced with **VEGETABLES.**

Sword fighting would be with **CUCUMBERS.**

CUCOMBAT

3. MOATS around castles would have been replaced with huge BALL PITS. And instead of having BOILING OIL poured on them, intruders would have received a refreshing shower of CABBAGE SOUP. Mmm, what a delicious, welcoming treat!

4. JOUSTING? NO, NO, NO. Instead, put oranges on the ends of those sticks and replace galloping horses with very slow, giant tortoises—and JOUSTING becomes JUICING.

It may take a long time for the two knights (in their woolen suits of armor) to get to each other, but when they do, they'll be able to enjoy a refreshing glass of orange joust!

NOTE: jousting + juice = JOUST

5. You don't need a **DANGEROLOGIST** to point out the dangerous part of a **UNICORN**. But this can be easily solved with a **LARGE VEGETABLE**. Now say hello to the

UNICORN-ON-THE-COB.

6. Finally, **DRAGONS** should be left to do whatever they want. If one kidnaps the princess, it's very hard to see how your rescue attempt is going to end in anything other than a **BARBE-YOU** (a barbecue involving you) with a side order of chargrilled princess.

The only thing to say to a dragon who kidnaps a princess is **"BON APPÉTIT,"** as you sprint away as fast as you can.

Now, I think you'll agree, with these six simple steps I would have made a dangerous time in the past **NOT DANGEROUS AT ALL.**

Thank you.

What is it about dangerous idiots that make so many people think
    they are great? I can't believe how excited Katherine and Millicent
are about this Wurst fool.

This is the same reason why I never go to the movie theater. Because
    every film is full of **INCREDIBLY DANGEROUS PEOPLE!**
  Everyone is half a bat, or half a spider, or some kind of
     wolf thing.

NO, THANK YOU VERY MUCH.

So I've used my Level 5 **DANGEROLOGY** skills (**NOTE:** I am the
  world's only Level 5 **DANGEROLOGIST**—thank you) to think up
   some safe **BUT STILL VERY EXCITING SUPERHEROES**
  that I'm hoping will become even more popular than the old, awful,
     dangerous ones.

Welcome to

THE LEAGUE OF EXTRAORDINARILY SAFE SUPERHEROES

BUBBLE-WRAP GIRL

All superheroes need a good tale of how they became a superhero. **BUBBLE-WRAP GIRL** fell out of her stroller when she was a baby, but **LANDED IN A PILE OF BUBBLE WRAP.**

Now she goes around wrapping up dangerous things in Bubble Wrap. You never know where she'll turn up next!

AT A RESTAURANT

AT A ROCK CONCERT

AT THE TENNIS CHAMPIONSHIP

THE COUCH

He once spent a terrifying night trapped inside a sofa bed that had closed on top of him. Now, whenever **THE COUCH** sees anyone who is standing up, cushions pop out of his arms and legs and he turns into a comfy seat.

NOTE: Standing in line is very difficult for **THE COUCH**. He has to tell people to get off him a lot.

DOCTER ZOEL NONE

The bravest and safest superhero of all, he is always dressed
in his ultra-cool superhero uniform. Nobody realizes it, but he
is secretly working behind the scenes to make everyone's life
MUCH LESS DANGEROUS. With the help of his loyal sidekick,
Lennis, he hopes to one day defeat his idiot nemesis,

WURSTMAN.

Then maybe he can get the beautiful Tretel to stop by his home.

A BIG JOB FOR DENNIS

This morning, as I lay in my bed/bathtub, I thought I was having a nightmare. A really scary one in which a giant Napkin had picked up **THE DANGERZONE** and was blowing into it like a whistle.

Then I realized the sound was coming from the living room, where I found that Napkin had chomped on the television remote control until she'd managed to find her favorite show.

NOTE: This never happens with a pet stone.

In this episode, Wurst and that slimy snake were at the top of a snowy mountain about to snowboard down while

**BLINDFOLDED
<u>AND WITH ROCKETS</u>
<u>ATTACHED TO HIS BOOTS.</u>**

"Noodle and I aren't going to get snow-bored on this snowboard! Isn't that right, Noodle?" Noodle didn't react and just dangled there, looking snakey.

Just then there was a sound from the front yard.

DING-A-LING!

DING-A-LING!

It was my mailbox alarm telling me the mailman had been there.

A question I'm sure you have right now is:

WHY DOESN'T THE WORLD'S GREATEST DANGEROLOGIST HAVE A MAIL SLOT IN HIS FRONT DOOR?

GOOD QUESTIONING!

All Level 2 **DANGEROLOGISTS** should be aware of
HOW DANGEROUS MAIL SLOTS ARE.

MAIL SLOT DANGER

A mail slot is like a small, always-open gate with a flashing sign over it that says:

SO MANY dangerous things can get in through your mail slot, including:

1. THE SNEAKY-BEAKED FLAMINGO

A rare tropical bird with a very long bill that flies up to houses, sticks its beak in through the mail slot and fishes out whatever it can find—usually keys, gloves, and umbrellas. Then it flies away, wearing these items as stylishly as possible.

2. THE CUSHION-EATING PACKAGE TOAD

This extremely smart and sneaky creature writes a random address on its back with its inky tongue, then inflates itself to look like a package and hops into the nearest mailbox. When the mailman delivers it, it chomps all the cushions it can find, before climbing out and mailing itself off again.

3. CHUBBY WASPS

The **WORST** wasps of all, and that's saying something. Look how four of them use their tubby bellies to hold the mail slot open while another ten swarm inside to eat all your cookies and treats.

4. PARP DONKEYS

The most awful of all the mail slot intruders.

THE PARP DONKEY doesn't even try to get into your house. It roams the streets late at night, searching for a mail slot that is at just the right height. It then reverses toward it, holds the mail slot open with its tail and aims a **COLOSSAL FART INSIDE.**

They are not particularly loud farts—you could easily mistake one for a creaky floorboard. No, the problem is

THE STINK.

A big cloud of it fills your home. You'll have to move out for at least a week while it wafts away. And then you'll need to repaint the whole place. **THEY ARE THAT BAD.**

TOP FIVE WORST FARTERS IN THE WORLD

ABSOLUTELY AWFUL STINK

VERY BAD STINK

STINK

Human dads—the sneakiest farters, they will often try to blame it on someone else, like the dog/you.

Bum-jet penguins—they power themselves through the water with their own farts, much to the anger of nearby fish and whales.

Whiffy hippos—
capable of the
dreaded "three-
minute fart."

Vampires—the
vampire honk can be as
loud as an airplane
taking off.

Parp donkeys

When I put on my **DANGER GLOVES** and **GOGGLES** to see
what had been left in the mailbox, I was disappointed to find a
flyer for that stupid pet competition.

ONLY FIVE DAYS
UNTIL
PET-OF-
THE-YEAR

Hosted by

"THE BRAVEST
MAN ON EARTH"

MAX WURST

But as I went to put it into the recycling bin, from over the wall next door I heard the most beautiful voice of all voices. A voice so beautiful it could tell you the worst news you'd ever heard and you would just laugh and think, "That is a beautiful voice."

Gretel was on the phone.

"It would be an honor to present the trophy! And I'll personally deliver one hundred cabbages to the home of the winner, too."

A trophy? And cabbages personally delivered by Gretel? Whatever this was sounded like the greatest competition **EVER**.

"Ethel loved winning last year. She still wears the hat from her country-and-western dance routine," Gretel went on. "But it's someone else's turn now. And I'm sure Max Wurst will be a great host."

Gretel was talking about Pet-of-the-Year!

If she was presenting the trophy, I couldn't run away and hide. . . .
I would have to talk to her!
Suddenly, entering didn't seem like such a terrible plan.

IT SEEMED LIKE THE BEST IDEA IN THE WORLD!

I dashed back inside and shouted:

DENNIS!
It's time to teach
an old stone some
new tricks.

CRUNCH FLAKES

CONGRATULATIONS!

On being over halfway through this book and halfway to becoming a

LEVEL 2
DANGEROLOGIST.

Time flies when you're having fun, but also when you are

LEARNING A HUGE AMOUNT OF VERY IMPORTANT DANGEROLOGY.

And you are certainly doing both of those things.

To celebrate reaching the halfway point and to take your mind off the **FRIGHTENING DANGEROLOGY** you have been learning about, and the **EVEN MORE TERRIFYING DANGEROLOGY THAT IS TO COME** (for example, the bit about the bus stop), here is a **VERY FUN** game for you to play.

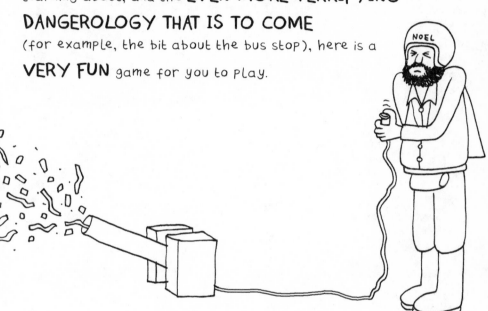

It is similar to Snakes and Ladders, but **LESS DANGEROUS.**

NOTE: Snakes = too slithery. Ladders = too wobbly.

I call this game . . .

FINISH!

Now you may continue reading **DANGER IS STILL EVERYWHERE.**

BEANBAGS &

24. GORDON Lands upside down, and you are trapped inside. **GAME OVER.**

23. A volcano explodes under your house. **LUCKILY** you are in **GORDON** and are blasted to safety. Move forward one space.

22. Fall off a ladder. But land on a beanbag! Move forward one space.

21

11. Your goldfish grows into a **GREAT WHITE SHARK** and chomps you. Start again.

12. You travel bac in time, but instead going to the spong age, you go to the Colosseum, dressed a gladiator. Miss turn.

9. You forgot about the **SPACE 9 SCORPION.** Go back one space.

10

8. Find your teacher hanging upside down. **UH-OH. VAMPIRE TEACHER!** Run back to the start.

7

6. A comfy beanbag! Snooze and miss a turn.

5. Find a dea bee in your cabbage sou Ugh. Start again.

MATTRESSES

The World's SAFEST Board Game

0. Go for a [swi]m. **UH-OH.** [you]r swimsuit is [mad]e of nettles. [S]tart again.

19. You are given a bicycle. Skip a turn while you throw it in a river.

18. It's your birthday! Move forward one space.

17

Gretel is much prettier than this.

16. See Gretel. **PANIC!** Hide in a tree and get kidnapped by an eagle. Go back to the start.

14. Giraffes steal your laundry. Go back three spaces.

15. Trip over a mattress. It's **OK**— have a power nap! Go forward one space.

13

3. Make delicious cabbage soup. Go forward two spaces.

2

1. Napkin turned on the tap in your bed. Go back to the start.

4

Rules:

1. You'll need a dice and two game pieces.

2. Sprouts (the smallest cabbages) make ideal game pieces.

3. A sprout with numbers stuck to it makes the perfect dice.

4. That's it.

START!

TRAINING BEGINS

"Have you been hit on the head by a giant cabbage?"
That was what Katherine asked when I told her that I was
going to try to win the P et-O f-The-Year contest with Dennis.

I had set up a blackboard in the kitchen and written all of
Dennis's talents on it. My nieces had come over to help me
choose the best one.

DENNIS'S TALENTS

1. Stops things from blowing away, for example, a trash can lid or a kite.
2. Holds doors open.
3. Makes a big splash when you throw him into water.
4. Very good at staying still/staring without blinking.
5. Excellent at impersonating other stones.

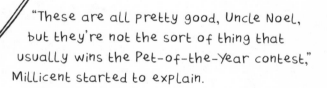

"These are all pretty good, Uncle Noel, but they're not the sort of thing that usually wins the Pet-of-the-Year contest," Millicent started to explain.

Katherine went on, "Mrs. O'Reilly from the dry cleaner will be entering with her pet bee, Bublé. He can land anywhere on a map of the world and buzz the national anthem of that country. Even really hard ones like Iceland and Paraguay."

Wow. That **WAS** very impressive. Dennis and I had a lot of work to do.

"But there's something I don't understand," said Millicent. "I thought you were going to stay as far away from Max Wurst as possible."

"Ah, yes, well . . ." I was too embarrassed to tell them that I was really doing it to meet Gretel and not run away, so I said, "I think it would be a very good chance to show Wurst and everyone else that a stone is the best pet."

NOTE: This is also true. **STONES ARE THE BEST PETS.**

Napkin, meanwhile, did not like us paying all this attention to her new best friend. Since there was no episode of *Expect the Wur* on television to distract her, she was running in and out to

THE DANGERYARD, yap-yapping at Ethel and the giraffes and rolling in a muddy puddle.

When we looked around **THE DANGERZONE**, it was the messiest it had ever been.

"Come on, nieces! Let's get this place cleaned up!"

TTTFADIES

(Top Ten Tips For Avoiding Danger In Everyday Situations)

CLEANING AND TIDYING SAFELY

1. A **VITAL** part of tidying is mopping, especially when there are muddy dog prints everywhere. But be very careful:

MOPPING CAN EASILY LEAD TO SLIPPING.

Avoid this problem by wearing a **MOPPING ONESIE,**
an all-in-one mopping suit that turns you into a human mop.
Then simply roll around the room until the floor is clean.

NAPKIN, PLEASE! Get away from
Millicent. **SHE IS NOT A DOG!**

No, wait, **DON'T PEE THERE!**
Oh, Napkin . . .

YAP-YAP
YAP-YAP

2. Napkin loves to try and lick plates that had food on them. But washing the dishes (with its combination of sharp silverware, things that can smash, and slimy dish soap) **IS TOO DANGEROUS**. A much safer option is to attach all dirty dishes and cups to your underwater diving suit and go along to the nearest car wash. Everything should be dry by the time you stroll home.

3. Awful things that can happen while dusting usually involve:

A. A ladder/chair

B. Some dust

C. A sneeze

D. You falling off that ladder/chair

Instead, stay safe (and stylish) while dusting

with a pair of **DUSTING WINGS**.

Simply stand in the center of the room and flap as hard as you can.
This will blow all dust and cobwebs out from wherever they are.

WARNING: You will also blow everything else out from wherever it is, so watch out for anything that can break.

WARNING 2: Never wear your **DUSTING WINGS** outside, especially on a windy day.

WARNING 3: NEVER flap while turning in a circle. This could create a **TORNOELDO** inside your home, which could destroy everything.

NOTE: I have invented the word **TORNOELDO.**

Thank you.

4. Don't clean your floors **TOO MUCH**. This makes them shiny, and **SHINY IS EVEN MORE DANGEROUS THAN SLIPPERY.** Say good-bye to slippery floors by finishing every cleaning by spraying a can of fizzy soda all over it. This will give you a much safer, stickier finish. . . .

NAPKIN! STOP LICKING THE FLOOR. . . .

DON'T PEE AGAIN!

Gah. This never happens with a pet stone.

5. Never clean your windows! If they are too clean, **YOU COULD EASILY FORGET THAT THEY ARE WINDOWS** and try to stick your head out them. Ow. If your windows are **TOO CLEAN**, wipe them with the nearest sticky dog. Thank you, Napkin.

SKULL AND CROSSZONES ALERT

6. When tidying, **ALWAYS** beware of **THE CROCUUM**, a rare kind of **INDOOR CROCODILE** (from Belgium) that resides in dark corners of homes and **PRETENDS TO BE A VACUUM CLEANER**. That is until you grab its tail and start pushing it around.

NOTE: Crocodiles, like pretty much every other animal, do **NOT** like being pushed around on their faces.

From that moment on, the only thing **THE CROCUUM** will be cleaning up is **YOU.**

7. While dealing with vacuum cleaners, **BEWARE** of the button that makes the plug whizz back toward you.

What if the cable gets tangled **AND PULLS BACK SOMETHING YOU DIDN'T EXPECT?**

For example:

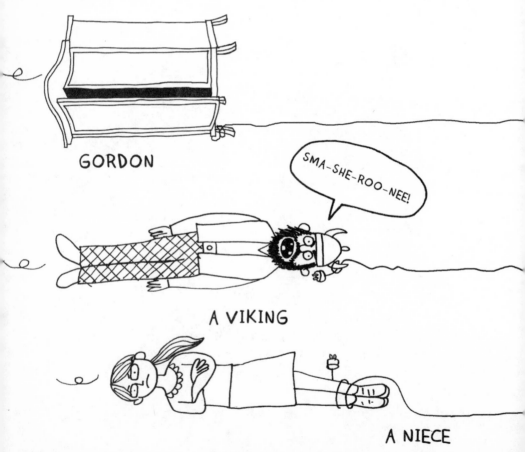

GORDON

SMA-SHE-ROO-NEE!

A VIKING

A NIECE

8. DON'T GET STUCK IN THE RECYCLING BIN.

This can easily happen if you climb into it to squash your recycling down. Be careful that the lid doesn't shut on top of you as

YOU COULD END UP GETTING RECYCLED.

9. Or **MUCH, MUCH** worse! On recycling days, look out for **THE HIPPOPOTABIN**, a sly hippo that waits outside houses posing as a bin . . . just until you open its mouth to put your trash in.

REMEMBER: Always

SAFBTB

(Stay Away From Bins That Burp).

10. Finally, when tidying with a chompy dog in your house, remember to put all chompable things in places where they **CAN'T BE CHOMPED.** Inside your fridge, for example.

NOTE: My fridge is called Roy.

WARNING: If you keep this book in your fridge, **DO NOT CONFUSE IT WITH A BLOCK OF CHEESE.**

DANGER IS ⟨STILL⟩ EVERYWHERE

is **NOT** good in a sandwich or on a pizza.

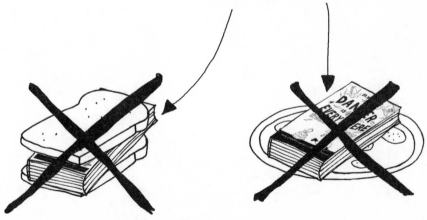

By far the most satisfying part of any cleaning is when you step back, look at your great work. . . .

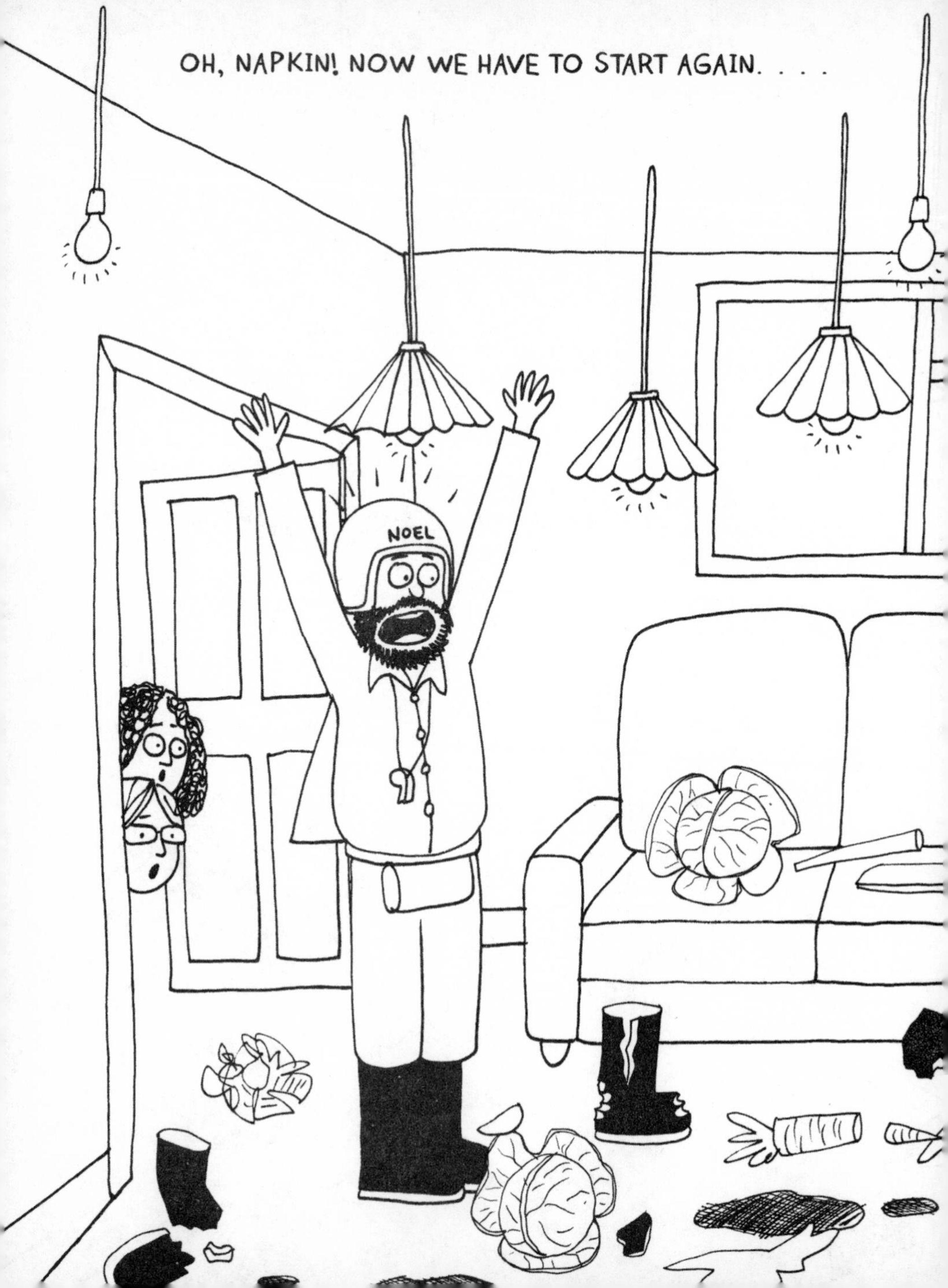
OH, NAPKIN! NOW WE HAVE TO START AGAIN. . . .
NOEL

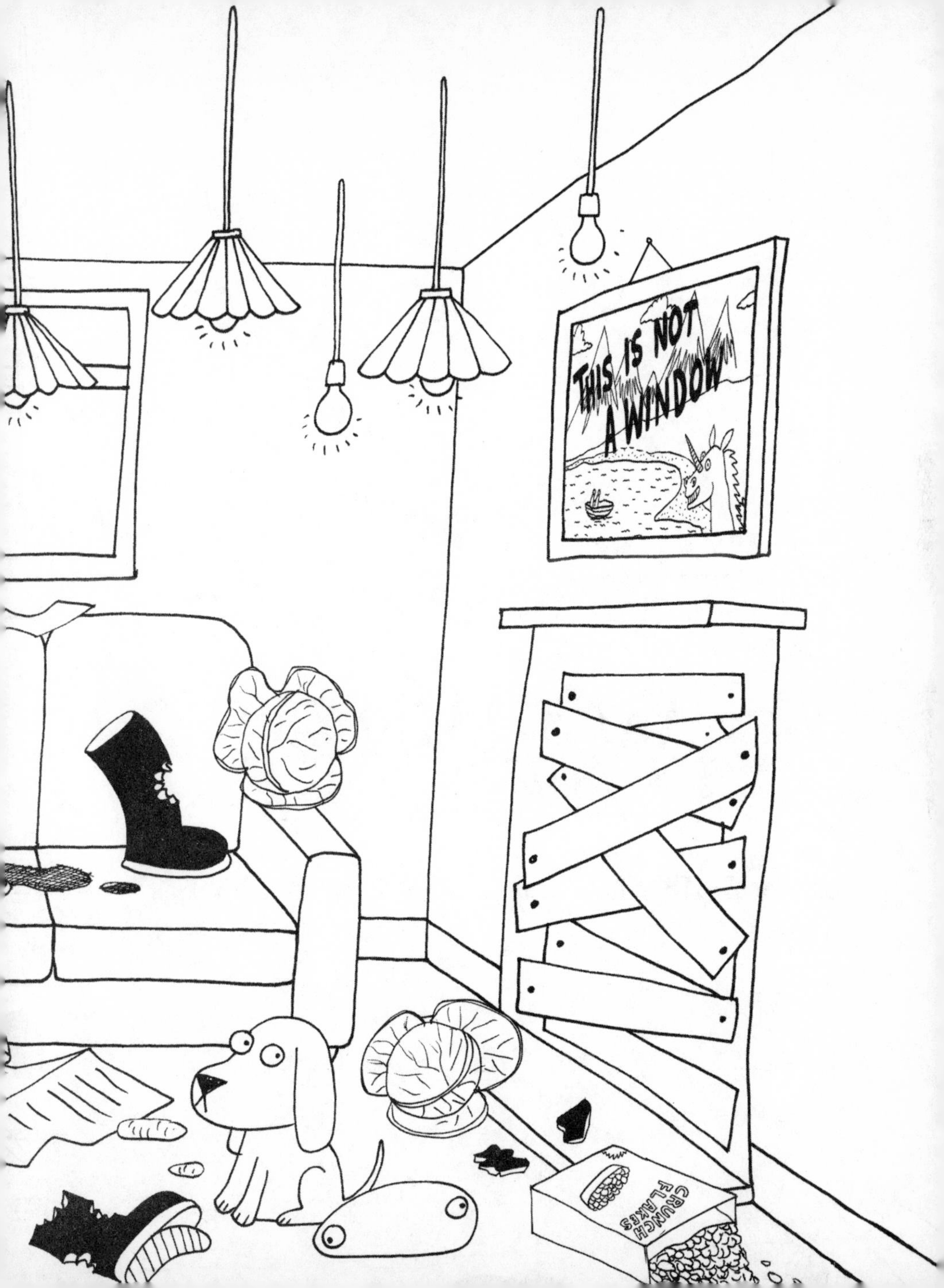
THIS IS NOT A WINDOW
CRUNCH FLAKES

WARNING!

WE ARE GETTING CLOSER TO PAGE 145.

Now, hopefully a ghost will **NOT** have gotten into your copy of this book. But if one has, **PLEASE DON'T BE SPOOKED!**

Thank you.

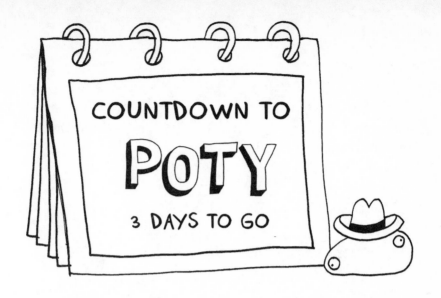

COUNTDOWN TO **POTY**

3 DAYS TO GO

NOT LIKE A ROLLING STONE

I was still struggling to think of something for Dennis to do at the contest. Katherine and Millicent had told me about some of the other amazing P et-O f-T he-Y ear entries.

Their neighbor Jane
would be entering with
her rabbit, Esther, who
could chop vegetables,
make noodles, and cook
a healthy stir-fry.

Demetri from the
ink-printer cartridge
shop has a hamster
called Grandmaster
Anthea who could DJ.

So I decided to take Dennis for a walk with Katherine, Millicent, and Napkin, to see if we could come up with an idea.

The problem with taking Napkin for a walk and trying to think is that it's very hard to think of anything other than Napkin.

WHEN OUT FOR A WALK WITH HER, THE MAIN THINGS TO AVOID ARE:

1. PEOPLE

Napkin gets **VERY** excited by every single person she sees. She wants to jump up on them and sniff them so much that her tail wags out of control and very often pee shoots out by mistake. Taking Napkin for a walk involves saying sorry

A LOT.

2. THINGS THAT *LOOK LIKE* PEOPLE

Not just actual people, Napkin also gets very excited by things she thinks might be people. These include statues, mannequins, pictures of people, trees that look like people, trees that don't particularly look like people, mailboxes, garbage bins, lampposts, and my shadow. There are just so many things to yap-yap at when you're Napkin.

3. DOGS

Napkin is on a mission to sniff every dog's bottom in the world. Unfortunately, for her, not every other dog in the world wants this to happen. Also, she seems to have no idea that she is a very small dog. So when she rushes, yap-yapping, toward every dog we ever pass, she is usually knocked over with one swoosh of their tail. But this doesn't stop Napkin. She gets straight back up and tries to sniff them again.

4. THINGS SHE THINK MIGHT BE DOGS

These include bins, bushes, bicycles, her own shadow, and her own reflection. She really doesn't like that.

5. SHOPS

Unlike Dennis, who sits politely on his roller skate, Napkin wants to investigate every shop, cafe, and restaurant she sees.

ESPECIALLY Alice's Cat-Grooming Palace, with all the fluffy cats that look like cream puffs in the window.

And the shoe store where I get my **DANGER BOOTS.** That would be Napkin's dream restaurant.

As we walked up the hill near the shopping center we saw Joey's Gelato van, but Joey did not look happy. She was standing behind her van, leaning all her weight against it.

"There's something wrong with the brakes, Docter Noel. I'm worried the van might roll away. Can you all help me lean against it until the mechanic gets here?"

"Of course we can!" I said, although Napkin seemed more interested in trying to jump inside Joey's van to eat all the ice cream. She was so excited she knocked Dennis off his roller skate.

CLOMP

"Wait!" I said. "Dennis can help!" I picked him up and wedged him behind the back wheel of the van.

Now there was no need to lean against it. . . .

DENNIS HAD SAVED THE DAY!

When the mechanic arrived, Joey gave us all delicious
ice creams to say thank you.

"Good boy, Dennis!" Millicent said. "Now we just have to
discover one more of your hidden talents before Saturday!"

GAH. Level 2 **PODs**, I really must apologize. Napkin and this contest are taking up so much of my attention here and we still have a **HUGE** amount of **DANGEROLOGY** to get through before the **Level 2 DETBAFOD**.

All this walking Napkin has reminded me about another Top Ten Tips For Avoiding Danger In Everyday Situations, this time dealing with something we all know very well.

TTTFADIES: <u>TRAVELING</u>

Visiting new places can be fun, but getting there can be
INCREDIBLY DANGEROUS.

Follow these excellent tips to make traveling **MUCH** safer.

1. There's nothing worse than getting on a full train and having to stand for the whole journey. Get around this problem by wearing this handy **SUITCASE ONESIE** and lying up in the overhead baggage rack instead.

2. Avoid annoyingly chatty people coming to sit beside you on the bus with an **INFLATABLE DOCTER NOEL ZONE**. He will provide excellent company, and you can use him as a pillow if you fall asleep.

NOTE: Similar to the book disguise earlier, **PLEASE DON'T USE HIM IF I AM AROUND.**

NOTE 2: DEFINITELY don't use him if Gretel is around.

3. Never ride a bicycle. Ever.

4. On all forms of transport it is vital that you have your ticket close at hand. I like to stick mine to the front of my **DANGER HELMET**. This means I can fall asleep and the ticket inspector doesn't have to wake me.

WELCOOOME TO PAGE
OOOOOOONE
FOOOOUR FIIIVE

5. Let me remind you again, **NEVER, EVER RIDE A BICYCLE.**

NOOOEL

ALWAAAYS TRAAAVEL BYY GHOOOOST TRAAAAIN. HAHAAAHAAA!!!!

6. I _____ an airplane. If you do, blindfold _____ aalm sounds of _____ your headphones.

NOTE: Not when Napkin is there, because that is mostly yap-yapping.

145

TIIIP SEEEEVEN IIIIS THAAAT YOOU SHOOOOULD JUUUUST FLOOOOAT LIIIKE A GHOOOOST.

7. Once again, do the same thing to any bicycles you do to pop-up books. BURY THEM IN A VERY DEEP HOLE.

8. If yo ___ as a ___ an urb ___ o syst ___ walk ___ statio ___ to stay away fron ___ hoever uses it.

9. Beware of Segwa ___ se
that person is de ___
Remember
MWAHAHA ___ HA!

10. When traveling by air, I always like to wear my own parachute. Just as when traveling by boat, I like to go one step further than a life jacket and **WEAR A BOAT OF MY OWN.**

OH MY GOODNESS. I completely forgot to warn you again about page 145! Oh well, we've passed it now and hopefully those ghosts didn't get up to any of their scary tricks in your copy of

NAPKIN GOES FISHING

"Please explain one more time what we are doing," said Katherine as we stood in our **DANGER HELMETS** beside the see-saw in the park.

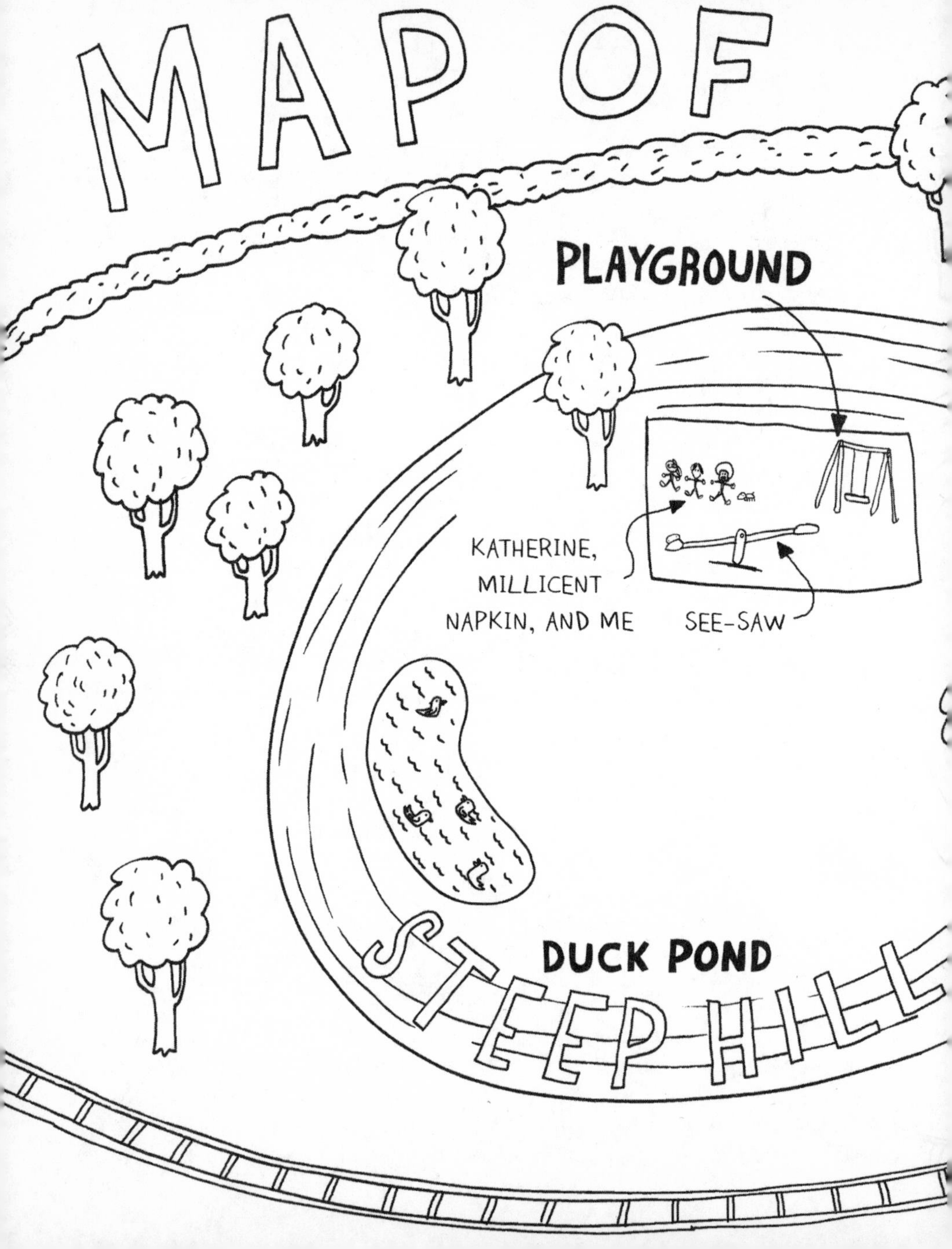
MAP OF
PLAYGROUND
KATHERINE,
MILLICENT
NAPKIN, AND ME
SEE-SAW
DUCK POND
STEEP HILL

THE PARK

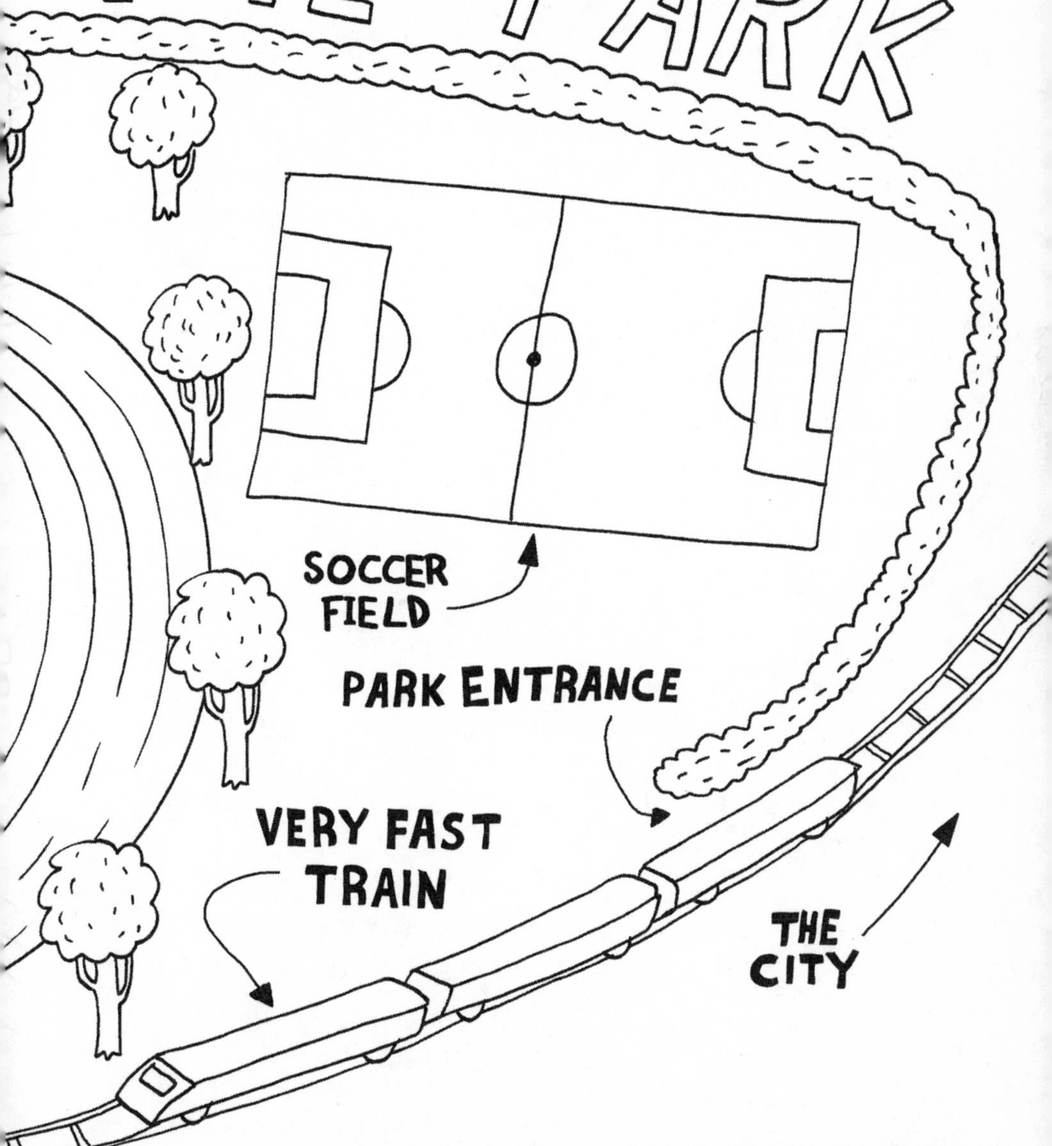
SOCCER FIELD
PARK ENTRANCE
VERY FAST TRAIN
THE CITY

LET ME SHOW YOU WHERE WE ARE IN THE PARK.

"I've made Dennis a pair of wings, so I'm hoping he will fly around the park, like an eagle. A big, lumpy eagle. We just have to jump onto the see-saw at the same time to get him up into the air."

"It seems a bit, I don't know, dangerous," said Katherine.

"Please, Katherine. I am the world's greatest **DANGEROLOGIST.** And we are all wearing our **DANGER HELMETS.**"

Napkin did not like what was happening to her new best friend. I'd tied her to the branch of a tree, but she was yap-yapping and pulling at her leash.

"Three, two, **ONE!**"
We leaped onto the see-saw, and Dennis took off into the sky.

"Now fly!" I yelled. But Dennis wasn't listening. He fell and landed

SPLASH

in the middle of the duck pond.

I was starting to worry about how we'd fish him out, when I got distracted by a dog in the distance that reminded me of Napkin. It was running toward the pond.

"It's so inconsiderate that people let their dogs off their leashes in the park," I said to Katherine and Millicent. "I bet it will come over here and Napkin will want to sniff it and there'll be a big kerfuffle. Isn't that right, Napkin? Oh."

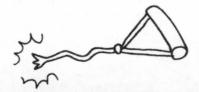

"NAAAAAPKIIIIIIN!" Katherine shouted as the three of us sprinted after her. I was worried that she might go out the main gate of the park or, even worse, run down the hill toward the train tracks.

But Napkin had only one thing on her doggy mind. With a final, mighty bound, she jumped into the pond to rescue her new best friend.

Millicent was the first to reach the water.

"NAPKIN, COME BACK HERE NOW!" she shouted as the ducks and swans went flapping up into the sky. But Napkin wasn't paying attention to them or us. She was paddling toward Dennis.

Then Napkin did a most extraordinary thing. She dipped under the water and emerged with Dennis balanced on her nose.

"Wow," said Millicent.

Before we had time to wonder if we had all just imagined it, she did something even more incredible—she flicked Dennis up in the air, **DID A BACKFLIP**, and caught him on her nose.

Then she did it again, this time catching him **ON HER TAIL**.

Some passersby who had seen her jump in began to applaud. How had Napkin learned to do these tricks? How could she be such a troublesome hound on land, but a graceful seal ballerina in water?

I didn't know the answer to these questions. But I was certain of one thing: Dennis would now be entering the Pet-Of-The-Year contest as part of a **DOUBLE ACT**, with his sidekick, Napkin the dog.

Danger was Every-where

Let's once again wind back the hands of time to another era that could really have used a Level 5 **DANGEROLOGIST**.

NOTE: As I said before, I am the only Level 5 **DANGEROLOGIST** in the world.

Thank you.

PIRATES

These swashbucklin' troublemakers of the high seas would have acted very differently if **DOCTER NOEL ZONE** had been in chaarrrrge.

1. Let's start with the names. Pirates always had the most frightening names:

Redbeard the Violent

Furious One-Eyed Ann

Captain McSwishy-Cutlass

What if instead they had nice names like:

Polite Wendy

Long John Friendly

Captain Gerald the Baker of Delicious Croissants

Awwwwww.

2. Pirate ships looked **TOO SCARY**. I'd have made them travel around making duck noises on big inflatable ducks.

QUACK QUACK QUACK

Not at all scary.

3. Instead of taking over other people's ships and stealing whatever they wanted, with me in charge pirates would have sneaked onto boats late at night and left presents for other sailors.

"In case you're feeling homesick, here is some soup."

"we thought you might be cold so we knitted you a wooly sweater."

Awwwwww.

4. Instead of those annoying, squawky parrots, each pirate would have had a pet stone on his shoulder.

NOTE: It is possible to teach a stone to talk, but they can only say two words: "clomp" and "thump." And when I say "talk," I mean "make that sound when you drop them on the ground."

5. No burying treasure to dig up later—my pirates would have **PLANTED CABBAGES** that the whole crew could enjoy.

REMEMBER: CABBAGES = NATURE'S TREASURE

COUNTDOWN TO POTY
1 DAY TO GO

A ROCK AND A HARD PLACE

The weather had turned cold, but Dennis, Napkin, and I went to the park for one final practice.

For the first time, I was starting to feel nervous in my tummy. What if Napkin got stage fright and forgot how to swim?

What if she spotted
someone in the crowd
wearing **DANGER BOOTS**
and went off to chomp
them instead?

What if she was too
excited to meet
Max Wurst and
peed on him?

But then I thought about Gretel presenting me with the trophy
and stopping by with the cabbages. . . .

I'd set the table for two, with a carrot that looked
like a romantic candle in the middle **BECAUSE REAL CANDLES
ARE MUCH TOO DANGEROUS**.

Gretel is
much
prettier
than this.

On top of the hill, everything was being set up for **POTY**.
There was a huge stage beside the pond, and in front of that
was an enormous grandstand. Lots of people were rushing
around unloading equipment and setting up a big antenna to
broadcast the contest live on the radio.

"Let's practice!" I unclipped Napkin's leash and threw
Dennis into the pond. "Now fetch!"

The first strange thing was that I didn't hear the usual
splash when Dennis hit the water. And then, when Napkin

jumped in, there was just a thump and a **SQUEEEEEEAK**.

I ran over and, instead of seeing Napkin the graceful
seal-dog bobbing through the water with Dennis balanced
on her nose, I saw Napkin the cold and confused dog
sliding across a layer of ice that covered the pond.

"OH NO!"

I picked Dennis up,
apologized to him in
advance, and tried to
bash a hole in the
ice with his slightly
pointier corner.

But it was no good.

"It'll be at least three days until that melts, maybe more," said a
man carrying a box of cables.

"WHAT?" I said.

"Oh, don't worry. We'll still have the contest.
There'll just be no feeding the ducks."

"Oh no! No, no, no," I said. "Can't we melt it?
I need it for my entry."

"That pond is frozen solid. Maybe you should teach
your dog to ice-skate on it."

The man laughed to himself as he walked away.

That was it. Our contest was over. No trophy,
no cabbages, no Gretel.

Napkin skidded back across the ice. She wasn't yap-yapping anymore. She was making a whimpering sound I'd never heard before. And when I picked her up, she was shivering.

I wrapped her in my **T-COD**, tucked her into my **DANGER ONESIE**, and with Dennis back on his roller skate, set off for home.

A group of people were standing on the stage as we walked past. One of them was very loud.

WHAT? Now I find out there's a zoo across the road from this dump? What if something escapes and tries to get me? I'd better be getting paid **A LOT** for whatever this is. Ugh, this coffee is disgusting. Get me a double shot of my own signature Max Wurst blend from my limo, and when you get back, you're fired. **WAIT.** Give me your scarf first. . . . No, wait. Give me all your scarves or you're all fired.

So I had finally come face-to-face with the bravest man on Earth, and he was an even bigger idiot than I thought possible.

And then he spotted us.

Wait. Look at this pizza-delivery guy with a rock on a string. Is that what passes for a pet around here? Probably does if you're a loser like him!

HAHAHAHA!

I didn't stop. I just wanted to get Napkin home to warm up, and then go to bed to end this awful day.

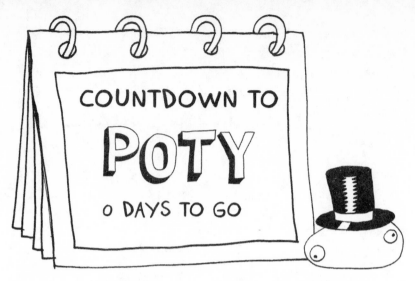

COUNTDOWN TO POTY
0 DAYS TO GO

Napkin was back to her old yap-yapping self, so Katherine, Millicent, and I took her and Dennis for a walk along the beach.

Although I was still feeling down in the dumps, I needed to be **ON HIGH ALERT FOR DANGER**. There is one seaside animal **EVERY** Level 2 POD should know about:

AAAAaAAA

THE HEADPHONES CRAB

Everyone loves a walk on the beach. It can really cheer you up when you've gotten bad news. The fresh air, the sound of the sea, the waves lapping around your **DANGER BOOTS**.

NOTE: NEVER PADDLE IN YOUR BARE FEET!
PADDLING IN YOUR BARE FEET IS LIKE
GOING INTO A GORILLA ENCLOSURE AT THE
ZOO DRESSED AS A BANANA SPLIT.

You never know what you're going to find walking along
the beach. Sometimes a nice shell, or even a new pet stone.
Maybe an old shoe that was washed off a ship far out at sea.
Or what's that? A pair of headphones?

They look great! They'll be perfect
for listening to my favorite
musAAAAAAAAGH. . . .

NEVER PUT ON HEADPHONES
YOU FIND AT THE BEACH.
YOU DID NOT FIND
HEADPHONES. YOU FOUND
A HEADPHONES CRAB.

Let me explain something. A lot of the animals I warn people about are sneaky.

They lie in wait for **YOU**.

THE LAPTOP CLAM, for example, is a rare oyster that looks like a **LAPTOP COMPUTER.** It waits in places you'd expect to find laptop computers: in offices and libraries.

Just until you start to type on it, then **CHOMP.**

NOTE: Also beware of the **LAPTOP CLAM'S** cousin, **THE PIZZA-BOX CLAM.**

But some dangerous animals aren't sneaky. They just happen to look like things you want to pick up.

THE SMARTPHONE BEETLE

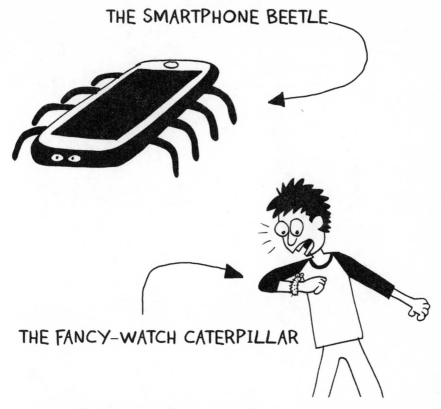

THE FANCY-WATCH CATERPILLAR

So it isn't **THE HEADPHONES CRAB's** fault. It doesn't know why people keep picking it up and shoving their hair in its face. But it doesn't like it. And when it doesn't like something, it has those big pinchy pincers to let you know.

YOU PROBABLY WON'T BE LISTENING TO ANY MUSIC FOR A WHILE.

A SPLASH OF LUCK

"Cheer up, Uncle Noel," Katherine said. "Auntie Joan is back tomorrow, and you've done a great job looking after Napkin."

"I suppose so," I said. But I was disappointed. Disappointed for Napkin, disappointed not to be showing everyone what a great pet Dennis is, and very disappointed that I wouldn't get to meet Gretel.

"You've discovered they both have amazing talents that nobody knew about," said Millicent. "Napkin in the water and Dennis stopping things from rolling away. That's great!"

"Can I see if Napkin brings back this stick?" Katherine asked.

I wasn't thinking straight. "Sure."

"WAIT . . ."

"NOOOOOO!"

But it was too late. Katherine had let go of Napkin's leash, and Napkin charged straight past the stick toward a huge flock of seagulls at the opposite end of the beach.

By the time I had caught up, hundreds of angry gulls were flying around Napkin, firing **FISH-STINKING BIRD POOPS DOWN ON HER.** I was very glad to be wearing my **DANGER HELMET.**

Back in **THE DANGERZONE**, Millicent switched the radio on to the **Pet-Of-The-Year** contest, while Katherine and I struggled to get bird-poopy Napkin into George the bathtub for a wash. Despite the excited cheers that greeted the start of the show, Wurst didn't sound pleased to be there.

Good morning or afternoon or whatever it is. I don't know how you people live in a freezing cow's butt of a town like this.

SOMEBODY GET ME ANOTHER COFFEE—I'm freezing up here.

So, while I wait for that, I'll introduce the first act of whatever this weird thing is. Clap as she comes on stage, some old lady called Mrs. O'Reilly and her pet—does that say 'bee'? Yes, a bee called Bublé.

Ugh, I hate bees.

As Bublé took his musical journey around the globe, we tried everything to entice Napkin into the warm soapy water: a cabbage, a cookie, even one of my last unchomped spare **DANGER BOOTS**.

Then Millicent had the right idea. She put Dennis into the bath and Napkin immediately jumped in beside him. Napkin looked around for a moment, as if she were thinking—something I'd never seen her do before.

And a second later she dipped under the water and emerged with Dennis balanced on her nose.

Then she tossed him up and caught him on her tail.

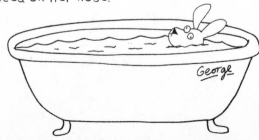

George

Soon she was swimming back and forth, as water sloshed everywhere in my bath/bedroom, doing new tricks. She skimmed along the water on her butt, holding Dennis in her front paws.

Then she seemed to bounce along on her nose, with her tail in the air, wrapped around Dennis.

She finished with Dennis balanced on her head, both of them perfectly still and staring at us as they sat on the edge of the bathtub.

"That was incredible!" said Millicent.

GET ME FOUR OF DENNIS'S OLD ROLLER SKATES, NAPKIN'S TRAVEL KENNEL, AND MY HAMMER. I HAVE A PLAN!

NOEL

Whoa! Wait! Let's not forget that we still have the **DETBAFOD** coming up, and there is one more **VERY IMPORTANT** piece of Level 2 **DANGEROLOGY.**

I would honk the **RAD HORN,** but unfortunately Napkin ate it earlier. So I'll squeeze it a few times. If you can just imagine some honking sounds, that would be great.

PFFFT PFFFT PFFFT

I'm sorry, but it's time for the really scary thing.

This one will separate the Level 2 **FODs** from the weren't-quite-brave-enough-to-get-past-being-Level-2 **PODs.**

WARNING!

AAAAaAAA

THE BUS-STOP COBRA

Here is a group of people waiting for the bus. It's early in the morning, so they're probably not fully awake. But I bet they're standing at that bus stop thinking to themselves that there's no danger around here.

OH MY GOODNESS!

THEY ARE SO WRONG!

THEY ARE MORE WRONG THAN THIS: 3 + 3 = 33

or this:

BAAAAA!!!

or this:

NEVER stand beside a bus stop that wasn't there yesterday.

NEVER stand beside a bus stop that is squishy or makes hissing sounds

Maybe just stay away from buses and bus stops in general.

NOTE: Don't get a bike, either. Just walk.

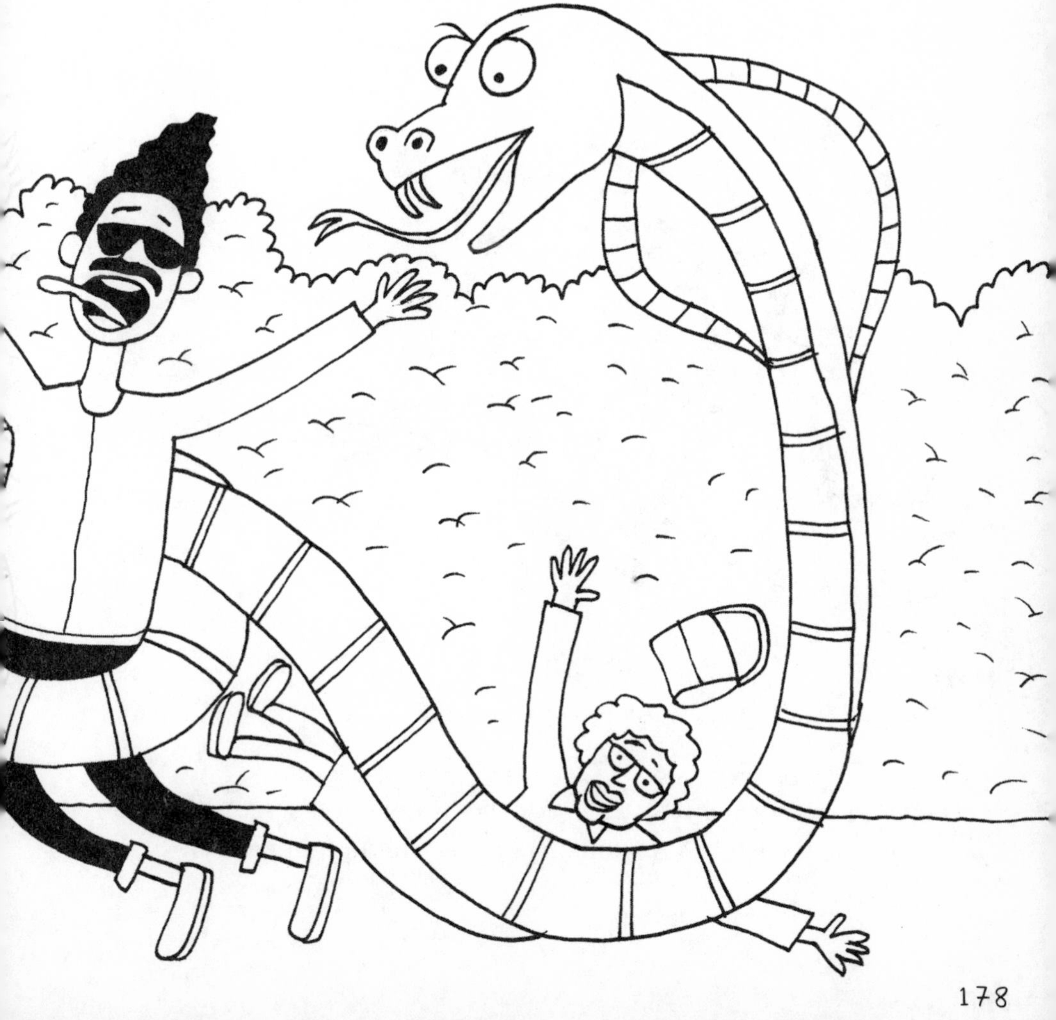

WURST-CASE SCENARIO

As I pushed George up the hill in the park, I could see people everywhere. My nieces followed close behind me, Katherine pulling Dennis, and Millicent carrying Napkin in her travel kennel.

Wurst was onstage, reading from his notes. And from the way people were hissing and booing at him, they'd had enough.

"So I've just been told that our final act—Chris and his dancing gorilla, David—has been disqualified from the contest because David's gorilla foot fell off, revealing that he is not a gorilla but a man in a cheap gorilla costume." Wurst threw his arms in the air. "That pretty much sums up this cheap gorilla costume of a town. The only good news is that I get to leave it now, while Mayor Whoever-He-Is picks the winner of this freak show."

"Hello!" I called out from the front of the stage. "I'd like to enter."

"Excuse me?" Wurst looked down and saw me.

"I'm Docter Noel Zone and I'd like to enter a double act: Napkin the dog and Dennis the stone."

Some of the crowd cheered.

"Oh, you're that crazy guy with the rock from yesterday. Well, too late, buddy. The contest is over."

Someone in the crowd shouted, **"LET HIM ENTER!"** And then somebody else did. Soon everybody was chanting:

"LET HIM ENTER! LET HIM ENTER!"

"**OK, OK**, fine, have it your way. Welcome to the stage, our final act, Mr. Norm Zoom, or whatever his name is, with a box and a rock."

As I walked up to the microphone, the whole crowd hushed, and the only sound I could hear was Katherine and Millicent behind me, pushing George onto the stage.

"Oh no! No, no, no!"

"Where is she? Can anybody see Napkin? I've lost her!"

"HAHAHA!" laughed Wurst. "Just when this contest couldn't get any worse, this human cannonball guy doesn't even have a pet!"

"We'll help you find him, Norm!" somebody shouted from the grandstand. And everybody cheered.

"Don't mind that Wurst guy," said someone else. "He's a real loser." And then everybody cheered again.

Wurst did not like this and began yelling back at them: "I'm Max Wurst. I'm the bravest man on Earth! I've water-skied behind a killer whale; I've done a rodeo on a walrus; I've eaten a boiled eagle's egg

IN FRONT OF AN EAGLE. . . ."

As he went through the long list of things he'd done,
I noticed Noodle dangling from his neck and had an idea.

It was a long shot, and it was **VERY DANGEROUS**. But it
was the only chance I had to find Napkin.

I crept forward, grabbed the snake's head, and blew into him as
hard as I could.

Max was furious. "HOW DARE YOU TOUCH NOODLE,
YOU BEARDY CLOWN. HE COULD HAVE
BITTEN YOUR HEAD CLEAN OFF OR
WRAPPED HIMSELF AROUND YOU AND . . ."

Wurst went on and on, but I wasn't listening. A cheer had gone up from the back of the crowd and a space began to open. Then a normally-annoying-but-this-time-**WONDERFUL** sound emerged.

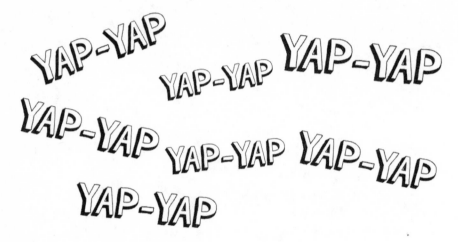

I saw Napkin's little face peeping out from a shredded green **DANGER BOOT** that she'd managed to get wrapped around herself, and for the first time in my life **I WAS VERY HAPPY TO SEE THAT DOG!**

When she noticed her hero standing onstage beside me, her eyes widened, her ears rose up, and a pee shot out from the other end.

As Napkin jumped onstage to meet Wurst, he stumbled backward, unaware that George was waiting there.

AAAAGH! IT'S A CROCODILE! NOOOOOO!

With Wurst splashing about, George started to move. . . . He rolled off the side of the stage, onto the grass, stopped for a moment at the top of the hill, and then began to roll down, building up speed as he went.

At first the crowd thought it was one of Max's dangerous stunts and cheered. But when they noticed the train coming along the railroad tracks at the bottom of the hill they went silent.

Wurst's assistants and security team were all yelling into their phones . . .

BUT NOBODY WAS DOING ANYTHING TO HELP.

So I did what any **DANGEROLOGIST** would have done in that situation. I picked Dennis up off his roller skate, put one foot on the skate, and pushed off down the hill after Max Wurst.

"Hello, Wurst," I said as I caught up with him.

"IT'S YOU!" he sputtered. His eyes had been shut tight, and his teeth were chattering. "Please help me, Zoom! I'm so scared!"

"I'll try," I said.

But I needed a plan, quickly. So I tried to think about this calmly.

You have something moving down a hill . . . .

How would you stop that?

With something that stops things moving down a hill.

And what stops things moving down a hill?

DENNIS!

There wasn't time to apologize to my pet again. I just threw him directly in front of George and dived off the roller skate in the opposite direction.

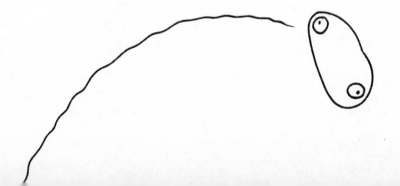

In a second it was over. George hit Dennis and stopped **IMMEDIATELY**, firing a screaming world's bravest man and a bathload of now very cold water into the air.

Wurst landed, skidded along on his belly for a while . . .

. . . and came to a stop in the muddy ditch just before the railroad tracks.

WHOOOOOSH!

A moment later, a deluge of cold bath water drenched him as the train to the city whizzed by safely.

A huge cheer went up from the crowd at the top of the hill, and they began to run down toward us.

"Are you **OK**?" I asked Wurst. I'd landed not far away.

"I'm very cold, but I think I am OK." Wurst looked miserable. He was covered in mud and had lost a shoe.

"Thank you, Zoom. I'm really sorry for being rude to you. Sometimes I'm an idiot."

I resisted the temptation to agree. "Not to worry," I said. "But I have one question."

"Yes?" he said.

"How do you wrestle tigers and surf on stingrays and do all of those things on your TV show, but you seem to be scared of every animal here?"

Wurst sighed. "That's all fake. You know, special effects, green screens, big rubber things. I'm scared of pretty much everything."

"I see. Well, sorry for blowing into Noodle," I said, pointing at the muddy snake next to him.

"Oh, he didn't mind. He's one of the rubber things," Wurst said. "You can have him. I have lots of spare Noodles in my limo."

As he threw me his rubber snake, his limousine skidded to a halt just beside us. Two of his assistants jumped out and started to help him in.

"I'd better go. You know, before the press sees me like this,"
he said, getting into the car. "I'm supposed to be the bravest
man in the world, and you were much braver than me.
Thanks again, Zoom, and sorry for, you know, everything."

I shrugged my shoulders and he drove off, just as
the crowd reached me.

"We declare that this year's Pet of the Year is Dennis,"
said the mayor, and the crowd erupted in cheers and applause.

Katherine and Millicent had found Dennis on the grass and
handed him to me.

Suddenly, photographers from the newspapers were
taking our photo.

I realized that I had completely forgotten about somebody else. "Napkin! Where's Napkin?"

From the crowd, Gretel stepped forward.

"Congratulations, Noel!" she said. "I'm Gretel."

"Thank you, Gretel," I whispered. "I live n-next door to you."

I couldn't believe it! I'd said something to her and did not run away!

"Great," said Gretel. "I'll drop by with the cabbages this week. . . ."

I didn't want this sentence to end, so I added: "And maybe you could stay for—"

Gretel added the last bit: "A cup of tea?"

"Yes!" I said.

"That would be lovely," said Gretel. "Although sometimes tea is a little hot for me."

"Me too! It can hurt your mouth," I said, nodding.

And then Gretel said, "I don't like dangerous things."

At that moment I felt so happy I could have fluttered my **T-COD** and taken off into the sky.

POTY
winner

Name: **DENNIS**

Variety of pet: **STONE**

Skill: **SAVING THE DAY**

Champion
PET
☆

NAPKIN'S LAST NIGHT

Napkin didn't want to watch Wurst sledding off an iceberg or whatever he was pretending to do on the television when we got home. This time she yap-yapped until I turned him off. She'd had enough of that guy. We'd all had enough of that guy.

I cooked us a delicious cabbage for dinner, and now, as Napkin happily chews on Noodle and Dennis sits on his trophy on top of the television, I will write the very last part of

DANGER IS STILL EVERYWHERE

Tomorrow, Joan comes to collect Napkin. And I won't give her the list I've been keeping of the many, many things her dog has chomped. I won't even mention the peeing or the yap-yapping. I'll just say, "If you ever need somebody to look after Napkin again, I'd love to do it."

I looked down and said to Napkin, "I'll miss you, little lady, and so will Dennis. But we'll come and visit. I promise."

For the first time ever, Napkin came over and sat on me, snuggling her head into my chest. And as she gazed calmly into my eyes, I felt a warm feeling I'd never felt before.

A moment later I realized that Napkin had peed on my lap.
I pushed her off, and she immediately started chomping my last
spare **DANGER BOOT.**

Oh, Napkin. This never happens with a pet stone.

I learned a lot from my time with a **DOG IN THE DANGERZONE**. But now we have to find out how much **YOU** learned from reading about it.

I HOPE YOU'VE BEEN PAYING ATTENTION, PODs, because now it's time for the:

LEVEL 2

DETBAFOD

Note: If you don't own this book, **YOU CAN'T JUST WRITE IN SOMEBODY ELSE'S COPY.** So go to lb-kids.com to print out your own **DETBAFOD** and **DOD.**

DOCTER NOEL ZONE

~Presents~

LEVEL 2

Dangerology Examination To Become A Full-On Dangerologist

- There are ten questions.

- Write your answer neatly underneath each question, or check the box.

- You will find the correct answers at the end—**NO CHEATING.**

GOOD LUCK, Level 2 PODs!

1. Which of these books is **THE MOST DANGEROUS?**

(a) Danger Is Still Everywhere ☐

(b) A how-to-train-your-dog book ☐

(c) A pop-up book ☐

2. What is the **SAFEST** thing to wear when traveling by boat?

(a) A sandwich costume ☐

(b) A boat ☐

(c) A pirate costume ☐

3. A big **PUDDLE** is blocking your way to school. What should you do?

(a) Try to jump over it. ☐

(b) Borrow a bike and ride through it. ☐

(c) Stay away from it and get a sea captain with a big harpoon gun in case there is something living in there. ☐

4. What is a sign that your home may be built on a **VOLCANO**?

(a) Giraffes stare at it. ☐

(b) Smoke is rising from the yard. ☐

(c) It's very cold. ☐

5. Which of these is a sign that your dog **MAY NOT BE A REAL DOG**?

(a) It walks around on its back legs making a sound like **UUUUUGH**. ☐

(b) It chomps your **DANGER BOOTS**. ☐

(c) It yap-yaps at Ethel. ☐

6. What is the **LAST THING** you should do to finish cleaning the floor?

(a) Polish the floor until you can see a reflection of your **DANGER HELMET** in it. ☐

(b) Rub a crocuum's face on it. ☐

(c) Open a can of fizzy soda over it. ☐

7. As well as being read, *Danger Is Still Everywhere* can also be used as:

(a) Cheese ☐

(b) A tiny island ☐

(c) A bathtub ☐

8. Which of these has the **STINKIEST** farts?

(a) Docter Noel Zone ☐

(b) The Parp Donkey ☐

(c) Dennis ☐

9. Who should you **NEVER SHY FIVE?**

(a) A Level 2 DANGEROLOGIST ☐

(b) A Level 5 DANGEROLOGIST (THIS IS ME) ☐

(c) This angry pirate ☐

10. What is **BY FAR** the most **DANGEROUS** page in every book?

(a) The first page ☐

(b) This page ☐

(c) Page 9 ☐

ANSWERS TO DEBTAFOD
(LEVEL 2)

1. (c) A pop-up book, of course!

2. (b) When traveling by boat, always wear a boat.

3. (c) Get somebody to deal with that **PUDDLE SHARK** before it chomps someone!

4. (b) But hope it's actually a barbecue and **NOT A VOLCANO.**

5. (a) Quick, get that **ZOMBIE DOG** to a vet!

6. (c) Open a fizzed-up can of fizzy soda, of course!

7. (b) But only if the flood is **VERY SMALL.**

8. (b) If anybody said (a), then **HOW DARE YOU!**

9. (c) Owwwwwwww.

FOR THE ANSWER TO QUESTION 10,
PLEASE TURN THE PAGE.

10. The answer is (c), of course—except if
you hide the page where it can't be found!

BETTER LUCK NEVER, PAGE 9 SCORPION!

You didn't find this page.

UNTIL WE MEET AGAIN.

Thank you.

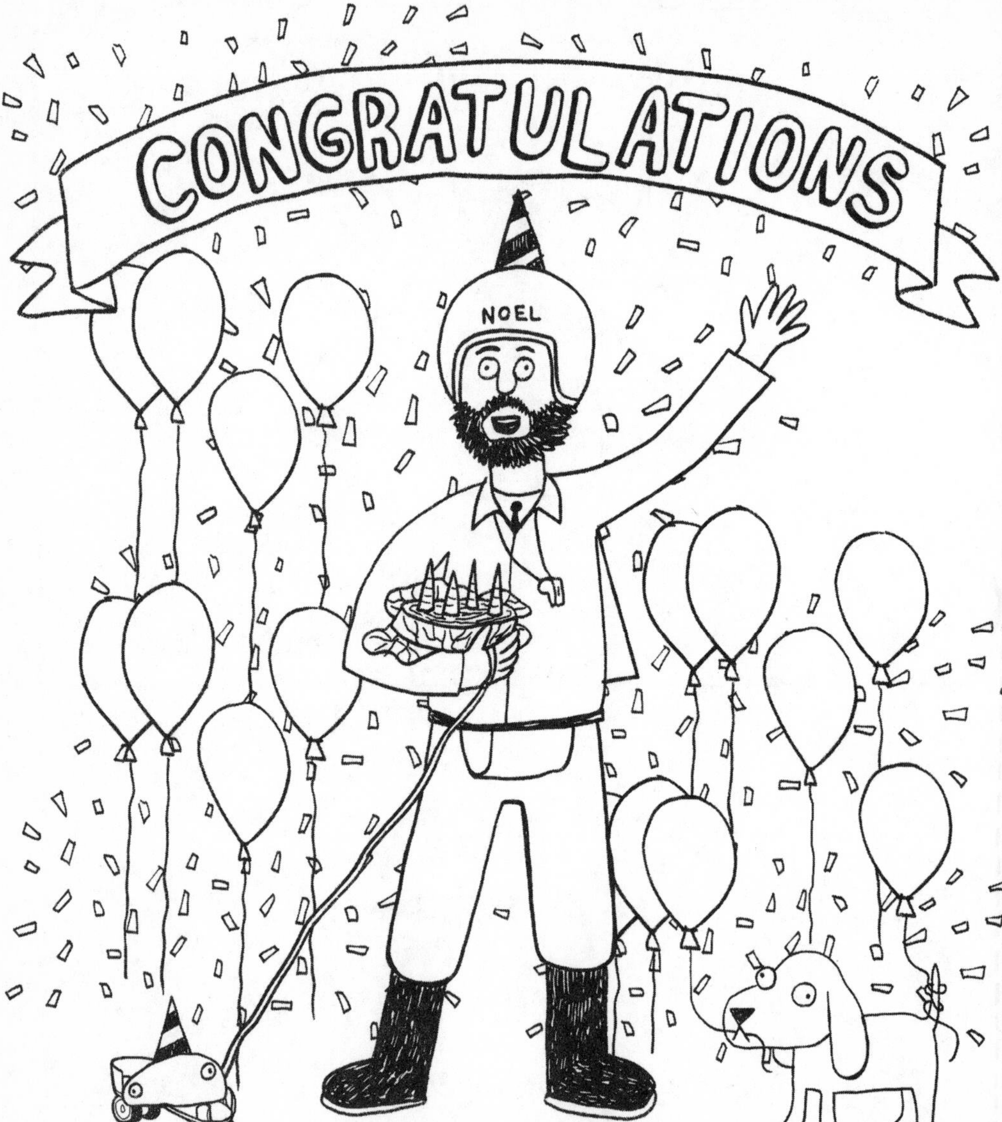
CONGRATULATIONS
NOEL

DOD (DIPLOMA OF DANGEROLOGY) Level 2

THIS IS TO CERTIFY THAT

DOCTER ....
(sign your name here)

has reached an excellent standard of knowledge in
BRABSE, Level 2 AAAAaAAA,
DANGER WAS EVERYWHERE, and Advanced **TTTFADIES**
and is now a qualified **FOD** (Level 2).

You can now rightfully **SHY-FIVE** other
LEVEL 2 DANGEROLOGISTS you meet.

Keep **LOFDing** (Looking Out For Danger)
and remember at all times that

D N Z
CABBAGE
OF
APPROVAL

Docter Noel Zone

DOCTER NOEL ZONE (Level 5)

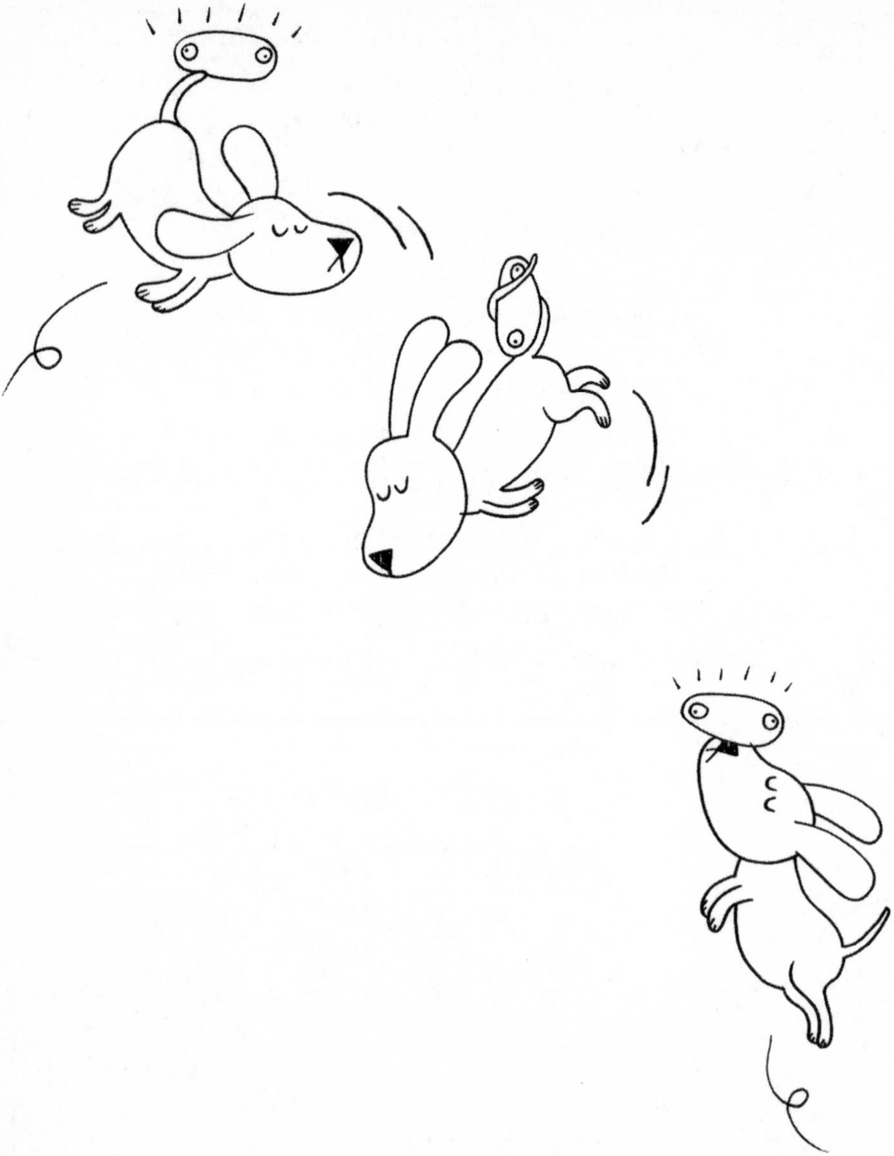

DANGER
~ IS {STILL} ~
EVERYWHERE

was written with
the help of my neighbors

DAVID O'DOHERTY (words)
and CHRIS JUDGE (pictures)

David →

 ← Chris

David O'Doherty is a comedian, writer, and regular guest on television shows such as *QI*, *Have I Got News For You*, and *Would I Lie To You?* He has written two theater shows for children, including one where he fixed their bicycles live on stage.

Chris Judge is the award-winning author/illustrator of *The Lonely Beast* and a number of other picture books for children. His recent work includes Roddy Doyle's novel *Brilliant* and a week spent in a cafe painting breadboards with pictures of animals that may never have existed.

They met when Chris was in a band and David used to come and watch.
They both live in Dublin, Ireland.

Pine River Library
395 Bayfield Center Dr.
P.O. Box 227
Bayfield, CO 81122
(970) 884-2222
www.prlibrary.org